COPPER AND SALT

MICHAELA GREY

Human trafficking is sadly all too real and it doesn't get talked about very much. You can visit the Polaris Project at https://polarisproject.org/ if you'd like to learn more about how you can help. This book is dedicated to those unseen victims and a portion of its proceeds go to Polaris.

1

——————

WHEN OREN ASHER stepped out his back door that brutal Cheyenne morning, the last thing he expected to find was a body sprawled on his porch, one arm outstretched as if reaching for the doorbell.

"*Shit.*"

Oren dropped the bag of trash he'd been taking to the can and crouched beside the body, rolling it carefully over to reveal a young man, his eyes closed. His skin hadn't frozen to the ice yet, which meant he hadn't been there long.

Oren didn't waste time trying to revive him outside. Instead he bent and scooped the young man up and into his arms in one quick motion, booting the door open and striding back inside.

His burden was horribly light, despite the fact that the young man appeared to be at least twenty years old, his hair blond where it wasn't matted down with dirt and blood. His skin was pale, veins standing out faint and blue as Oren cleared a space on the couch and laid him down to listen for a heartbeat.

It was there, faint and irregular but present, and Oren drew a breath of relief and grabbed the heavy throw off the back of the couch.

"You would pick the biggest ice storm of the year to be caught in," he said aloud as he gently bundled his guest into the layers. "Phone lines are down. Everyone in town is without power. Hell, pretty sure most of Wyoming is without power right now. I couldn't call emergency services if I wanted to." He paused. "Which I, of course, *do* want to."

The boy didn't stir, his head lolling and his eyes still closed as Oren wiped his hands on his pants, grimacing. His fingers felt tacky, sticky and dirty, and he suddenly desperately wanted a bath.

He eased back onto his heels and surveyed his handiwork. The young man looked like a human burrito, wrapped in the blanket as tightly as Oren could get him, and Oren chewed thoughtfully on his lip.

"Stay right there," he said.

He hurried for the bathroom and turned on the wall heater, then began to fill the huge claw-foot tub. He dug his first aid kit out from under the sink and then dashed back to the living room.

The stranger was still unconscious when

Oren gathered him into his arms and carried him up the stairs and into the bathroom. He set him on the floor in front of the tub and pulled back the layers of the blanket, grimacing at the filthy shirt revealed.

"I'm sorry about this, for the record," he murmured, and used the scissors from the kit to cut the shirt off.

He bit his lip until he tasted blood as he peeled the tattered rags away from bruised and torn skin. Most of the young man's torso was covered in lumps and contusions in various stages of healing, as if he'd been beaten on a regular basis. Even in his unconscious state, he seemed to curl protectively around his right side, and Oren felt carefully along his ribcage, hissing at the lump there.

"Looks like you've got some cracked ribs at least," he said. He wasn't sure why he was talking aloud, except that it seemed to lessen the weirdness of the situation, having a half-dead, almost naked stranger on his bathroom floor. "I'm gonna take your pants off now, okay?"

He eased the thin khakis down lean thighs purple and green with old bruises, breathing through his mouth and trying to remember how to pray. His *abuela* had taught him, once, but he couldn't quite bring the old rhythm to mind—the young man roused, opening dark brown eyes, and grabbed Oren's arm with startling strength.

"Mihai," he whispered, holding Oren's eyes.

"Is that… is that your name?"

The young man shook his head, panic in the set of his face, the tension of his shoulders. "Alex." His heels scrabbled against the hard tile floor as he tried to sit up.

"Okay, Alex," Oren said as soothingly as he could. "Easy. We need to get you warmed up, and when the phone lines come back, we'll call an ambulance. We're snowed in right now, but—"

"*No!*" Alex jackknifed away, colliding with the tub and making Oren wince in sympathy at the hollow thud. "No ambulance!" He was trembling as he pressed himself into the corner, thin shoulders against the wall, drawing his knees to his chest.

Oren held out a hand but didn't move from his position. "Okay," he repeated. "No ambulance. We do need to get you warmed up though, look how you're shivering, you see that?"

Alex looked down at himself, his eyes unfocused and vague, and didn't answer.

Oren inched a little nearer. "Come on," he coaxed. "You'll feel better once you're warm."

He kept his hand out, waiting, and finally Alex relaxed his grip on his knees and took the edge of the tub, ducking away from Oren's hand as he pulled himself upright.

Oren shuffled backward to give him room, staying close enough to catch him if he fell, and Alex stepped into the tub, hissing at the hot water as he sank into it. He drew his knees back up, turning his head away and resting his face against his knees as if indifferent to anything Oren might do.

There were fingerprint bruises on Alex's neck, Oren realized as sick horror wormed in his stomach, livid and distinct like a big hand had held him, pinned him down—Oren scrambled to his feet, willing himself to not throw up, and backed away.

"I'll… be right back," he managed, distantly aware that his voice was trembling, and bolted.

Outside in the dim hallway, he braced his hands on his knees and tried to breathe. *What have I gotten myself into?*

AFTER A MINUTE, he straightened and went back in. Alex didn't stir, and Oren realized that he'd fallen asleep sitting upright, leaning against the side of the tub.

"God, you poor kid," Oren whispered. He knelt and picked up a sponge.

Alex startled awake with a choked gasp when Oren touched his shoulder and Oren held up his hands.

"Just going to clean you up," he said quietly. "That okay?"

Alex eyed him, wariness rampant in his dark eyes, but finally he nodded once, wincing at the movement.

"You just hold still, I'll do all the heavy lifting," Oren said. He set to work, squeezing warm water over Alex's skinny shoulders and sluicing away blood and grime, leaving clean skin and yellowing bruises behind.

Halfway through, he stopped and drained the tub and refilled it with more hot water. Alex sighed, tension visibly leaving his muscles, and pillowed his head on his arms on the rim of the tub as Oren worked.

"That was a real humdinger of a storm, wasn't it?" Oren said, mostly to fill the silence. Somewhat predictably by now, Alex didn't answer. "Thank God I don't have to go out in it—well, much, anyway. I wouldn't have been out at all if I hadn't needed to throw out my trash, which is lucky for you. Otherwise you might have turned into a popsicle right there on my back porch."

"What is… popsicle?" Alex asked, his voice slow and burred with sleep. He had an accent, Oren realized, but he couldn't place it. European, he thought, but he couldn't be more specific than that yet.

"It's—oh, frozen juice, or ice cream, on a stick. Kids like to eat them in the summers," Oren said, easing Alex to the other side of the tub. "Very popular in the south—not as much up here, I guess."

Alex said nothing.

"Can you tilt your head back so I can wash your hair?"

Alex wordlessly obeyed, revealing a long, slender neck covered in more bruises, and Oren poured water over his head, careful to keep it out of his eyes. He worked the shampoo through the strands with gentle fingers, wincing every time Alex did, and then tilted Alex's head back again and rinsed the shampoo from his scalp.

When he was done, Oren was relieved to find that apart from a cut on his forehead, Alex didn't have any open wounds. An ambulance was not immediately necessary, he decided, sitting back on his heels. He was pretty sure Alex had fallen asleep again, dark lashes fanned out over pale cheeks and his mouth drooping downward in exhaustion and pain.

Which reminded him—Oren rocked to his feet and stood up to rummage in his medicine cabinet. He had some leftover narcotics from his appendix surgery the year before. He shook one out onto his palm and poured a glass of water before turning and stooping to the tub.

"Hey," he said gently. "Can you take this for me?"

Alex lashed out, smacking Oren's hand away with a snarled curse that definitely wasn't in English, clipping the glass with his elbow and knocking it out of Oren's grip. It shattered on the floor as Alex cowered backward, flinging his arms up over his head as if waiting for Oren to hit him.

Oren didn't move, stunned, staring at the puddle on the floor that was soaking into his socks.

"Okay," he said after a minute, his voice a little unsteady. "So maybe no drugs. You, uh… think you can get out of the tub? Wait, hang on, let me clean this mess up first."

He grabbed a towel and mopped up the worst of it, peeling off his wet socks and aware that Alex was watching him behind the crook of his elbow as he worked, careful to keep his motions calm and relaxed as a result.

"Stay there," he said when he was done. "I'm going to get you some clothes."

He was half-expecting Alex to be gone when he came back with a pair of sweats and long underwear, vanished like some strange hallucination brought on by too much Oscar Wilde and tequila before bed, but no, Alex was right where Oren had left him, clutching his knees and staring out the window.

Like before, Alex didn't accept his hand, gripping the edge of the tub and pulling himself to his feet. He wavered as he stepped out and Oren wrapped the towel around him quickly, using it as an excuse to prop him up as he dried him off and helped him step into the clothes.

"Hold onto my shoulder," he directed, and felt Alex obey, fingers light as butterfly feet against Oren's flannel shirt. When Oren was done, he straightened, face to face with Alex for the first time. He was a little shorter, he realized, Alex taller and thinner than Oren's sturdy five foot ten.

Alex swayed and Oren caught his elbow, alarmed.

"Can you walk?" he asked.

"To… where?" Alex slurred. "Siberia… no. Living room… maybe."

"Oh my god, you have a sense of humor," Oren said, delighted. "I like you already. I was actually thinking my bed." Alex slanted a look at him and Oren shook his head. "It's not like that. It's a one bedroom house, and the couch is terrible, all lumpy and miserable, but if you'd *prefer* to be on it…."

"Yes," Alex said firmly. "Couch." But when he put weight on his right foot, he nearly went down, and only a quick lunge by Oren saved him from sprawling.

"Sorry," Oren panted, letting go as quickly as he could. "Let me look at that ankle, I think I missed something."

Alex eased himself onto the closed toilet lid and Oren felt the joint, hissing through his teeth.

"It's swollen," he said. "My one summer as a lifeguard for the YMCA didn't really qualify me for this shit, but I don't *think* it's broken? I'd feel better if you went to the hospital and had an X-ray to be sure, though."

Alex jerked his foot out of Oren's hands. "*No.*"

"Okay," Oren said, scooting backward. "No one's going to make you do anything you don't want to do."

Alex's laugh was jagged, splintered, and it hurt something in Oren's chest.

Oren stayed close as Alex stood up, then motioned for him to put his arm around his shoulders. They made their way out of the bathroom and down the narrow hall to the landing, slow and limping, and then paused.

"Stairs," Oren said unnecessarily.

Alex said nothing, but his look suggested Oren might be a little brain-damaged. He breathed heavily through his nose and gripped the banister, taking the steps slowly as Oren kept pace.

When they were finally in the living room, Oren was a nervous wreck and Alex was trembling again.

"Let's never do that again," Oren said as Alex sank onto the cushions. Oren tucked the blankets around Alex's shivering body and felt his forehead. "I don't think you have a fever. Maybe we got lucky and you'll avoid coming down with anything. When's the last time you ate?"

Alex blinked, clearly trying to focus. "Two… days?"

"Two days ago?" Oren asked, horrified. "*Jesus*, kid. Okay, hang on, I'm going to get you something to eat. You just rest."

Alex closed his eyes, his mouth shaping a word silently. Oren couldn't be sure, but he thought it might be the same one he'd said when he'd come to in the bathroom. *Mihai.*

OREN WAS glad for the open floor plan of his house, the kitchen down a short flight of steps and the couch in plain view from the stove as he heated up yesterday's chicken soup.

Alex stayed huddled in place, a motionless ball under the blankets as Oren bumped and clanked in the kitchen, humming to himself as he worked.

He needed to call the authorities the second the phone lines were back up, he knew that, loath as he was to take that step. Alex was clearly on the run from something or someone, and whatever it was, Oren didn't want to get involved with that. It would be better for everyone if he handed the young man over to the police and let them take care of it, except for the spotlight that would turn on him.

Was there a way he could turn Alex over anonymously? Oren paused, spoon held above the saucepan, as he considered that option. Drive into town once the roads were clear, take Alex to the hospital and drop him off, maybe leave before they got his name?

No. Oren began stirring the soup again before it burned, shaking his head. Better to give it a day or two, let the ice melt, see if he could get some more information out of his guest about his origins. Maybe he had an innocent backstory and all this stress was for naught.

Oren snorted and poured soup into a mug. *And maybe Ryan Reynolds will leave Blake Lively for me.*

He climbed back to the living room with a steaming hot mug of soup, making sure Alex knew he was coming with deliberately heavy footfalls. He set the food on the coffee table as Alex stirred and sat up, behind him.

"Can you feed yourself?" Oren asked.

"Yes," Alex said quietly.

"Good. I'm going to get the first aid kit and wrap your ankle and ribs. The cut on your forehead needs to be bandaged too."

He left Alex to start eating and headed for the bathroom, spending a few minutes tidying up the wreckage before gathering the supplies he needed. Then he ducked down the hallway into his bedroom and grabbed one of his thickest pairs of socks before going back down to the living room.

Alex was already done with the bowl of soup, curled back up on his side with his hand tucked under his cheek, eyes closed. Oren knelt in front of him and opened the kit, taking out the antiseptic ointment and gauze.

"This is going to sting," he warned.

Alex said nothing, but his throat worked as he swallowed.

Oren dabbed the ointment along the cut on Alex's forehead, tongue caught between his teeth in concentration. Once it was dressed and bandaged, he touched Alex's shoulder.

"Can you sit up for me? We need to wrap your ribs."

Alex squeezed his eyes shut tighter and shook his head, pressing his face against the cushion.

Confused, Oren waited, but Alex didn't move.

"Come on," Oren coaxed, "sit up and after, you can have more soup."

Alex clenched his fists, a vein throbbing in his temple, and pushed himself upright. When Oren reached for his shirt, though, Alex shoved him away.

"*No.*"

"It's not like that!" Oren said for the second time. "I'm sorry, but I have to lift your shirt to get to your ribs to wrap them properly."

"Why?" Alex demanded, his brown eyes anguished.

"Because I'm pretty sure they're cracked," Oren said carefully. "Remember? We talked about this. Did you hit your head—"

"No, why...." Alex clutched at his hair as his English failed him and he lapsed into another language, round vowels and crackling syllables that spilled over in a rolling wave of sound. He covered his face after a minute and his shoulders shook. "*Mihai.*"

"That's the third time you've said that word," Oren said. He was still kneeling on the floor, far enough away that Alex hopefully wouldn't feel threatened by his presence. "Is Mihai a person, Alex?"

Alex lowered his hands. There were tears on his cheeks. "I have... no money," he said. "Why do you help?"

Oren stared at him for a minute as he considered and discarded several responses. *What other option is there? Basic human decency demands it. I couldn't exactly let you freeze to death.*

Finally he lifted a shoulder, smiling a little ruefully. "Will you at least let me bandage your ankle?"

Alex hesitated, then raised his leg, placing his foot in Oren's hands, his eyes steady on Oren's. There was a crystalline moment of silence as they looked at each other and then Oren bent to his task, unwinding the bandage and rolling it into place around the delicate framework of Alex's ankle, muscle and tissue stretched over bone like a fragile canvas.

When he was done, he tucked the ends in and smoothed them down with his thumb. "There," he said, smiling at his work. "All done." He grabbed the socks and eased them into place before glancing up at Alex, who was looking down at the clothes Oren had put him in.

Alex looked up, something like panic on his face. "Where are clothes?"

"The ones you were wearing?" Oren asked. "They're rags, I was going to burn them."

Alex made an inarticulate noise of protest, clutching at Oren's arm. "No, please, I need—"

"Was there something in them that you need?" Oren asked.

"Da, yes, in pocket," Alex said, his whole body taut and desperate. "Please, I need to—"

"Easy," Oren said, gently dislodging Alex's hand and getting to his feet. "I'll get it, okay? You just stay there. I'll be right back."

He jogged up the stairs to the bathroom and found Alex's filthy pants in a crumpled heap, digging through them with a grimace. In the right hand pocket, he found a folded piece of paper, but further probing turned up nothing else.

Resisting the urge to look at it, Oren returned to the living room and handed the paper to Alex, who very nearly snatched it from his hands, clutching it to his chest.

"*Mulțumesc,*" he whispered.

Oren bent to close his first aid kit. "Ready for that second bowl of soup?"

Alex nodded and Oren smiled at him and went to get it.

He busied himself cleaning up as Alex ate, keeping where Alex could see him and avoiding any loud noises.

Alex's head was back against the cushions of the couch when Oren finished, his long throat exposed and the bruises thrown into stark relief by the winter sun.

Oren closed his eyes briefly and then coughed, pretending not to notice the way Alex started at the noise.

"I'm going to be up and down the stairs, working around the place," he said as he picked up Alex's bowl and Alex watched him with wary eyes. "Don't mind me, just stay here and rest. If you need anything, just yell for me."

"What...." Alex chewed his lip briefly. "What is—name?"

"Oh *God*, I'm sorry!" Oren held out a

hand and then pulled it back almost as quickly, feeling like an idiot. "I'm… Oren. Oren Asher."

Alex nodded, and the corner of his mouth curved up a tiny bit as he closed his eyes again.

2

———

OREN SPENT a few minutes putting the kitchen to rights, sneaking surreptitious looks at Alex, who appeared to already be asleep again. Finally, though, he was ready to go downstairs and get to work.

He tiptoed past Alex's curled up form and down the stairs on the opposite end of the living room that led down into his pride and joy, the place he'd spent countless hours getting just right.

The polished mahogany banister gleamed, curving in a graceful arc around three of the four walls below. He'd carved most of the space from the rock himself, camping out in a small Airstream as he painstakingly built his workshop and home, living on dime store noodles and peanut butter and scrimping and saving every penny he could get his hands on.

Oren trailed a hand along the banister, smiling to himself. Even dimly lit with only the weak sunlight from windows overhead, the room glowed with a soft welcome.

He hopped the last two steps and ducked left around a towering bookcase, heading down the narrow path that led to his tiny office tucked away in the back.

The workshop wasn't very big, but the stone of the hillside it had been built into swallowed sound, and Oren wanted to be able to hear Alex if he called, so he gathered his files and headed back up the stairs, his arms full.

Alex was asleep again and didn't stir as Oren settled in at the little kitchen table, spreading the documents across the flat surface and getting to work.

Several hours passed, the house silent except for the crackling of the fireplace and their breathing. Oren got up several times to add more wood, checking on Alex each time.

As the sun began to set, Alex sat up and stretched. Oren noticed and put his pen down.

"Hey, how are you feeling?"

Alex ducked his head and mumbled something.

"Are you hungry?" Oren asked, standing. "I can heat some more soup, or make you a sandwich, or—"

Alex looked up. "I need—" He hesitated. "Bathroom?"

"Oh my God, I'm an *idiot*," Oren exclaimed. He hurried up the stairs and held out his hand to Alex, who took it and allowed

Oren to pull him to his feet. "I'm so sorry, I'm a terrible host."

Alex said nothing as he wrapped an arm around Oren's shoulders, but his mouth curved up slightly.

They hobbled haltingly up the stairs to the landing, where they paused so Alex could catch his breath.

"Doing okay?" Oren asked. "Are you sure you wouldn't rather I just carried you?"

"Can walk," Alex said.

"Donkey," Oren said under his breath. Alex shot him a startled look but didn't comment as they tackled the second short flight of stairs.

At the bathroom, Oren stopped and Alex slipped inside, shutting the door behind him. Oren leaned against the wall and waited, wondering if Alex was going to climb out the window and escape. Not that he'd get very far if he tried that—the bathroom looked out over a craggy outcropping of rock and a twenty foot drop to the base of the hill below. Alex would have to be a mountain goat if he wanted to go that route.

After a few minutes, the toilet flushed and then the sink ran. Alex appeared, his face pale, and Oren jumped forward to steady him.

"Getting to be dinnertime. Let's get you back to the couch and I'll whip something up for us. Too bad I don't have power right now, or we could watch a movie. I guess we'll just have to read, or make conversation like civilized people."

Alex's breathing was harsh but his lips twitched. "My English… not good."

"Hey, no problem," Oren said easily, steadying him down the steps. "You may not have noticed, but I like the sound of my own voice."

"I… noticed," Alex managed, collapsing onto the couch.

Oren laughed. "Alright, you rest, I'll be right back."

They ate in the firelight, bowls of beef stew balanced on their knees and a plate of garlic toast between them. When they were done, Oren gathered the dishes and took them to wash. He spent a few minutes cleaning the kitchen in the flickering candlelight and then climbed back to the living room.

Alex gestured at the stairs and made a motion with his hands. "Is good—for muscles, living here? Much… climb."

Oren laughed. "You could say that. I like it, though. Keeps me fit." He wavered for a minute and then sat down, fixing Alex with a serious look. "So I've been thinking."

Alex's face shuttered and he hunched his shoulders, withdrawing into himself without speaking.

"I know you don't want to be here," Oren said. "To be honest, I really don't want you here either." Alex shot him a startled look and Oren smiled, a little rueful, but didn't elaborate.

Alex opened his mouth and then closed it again, nodding.

"Anyway," Oren continued, "my point is, we both want you gone, but that's impossible at the moment. I'm frankly amazed that you got as far as you did on that ankle. But the ice isn't going anywhere and we're in for some bad snow next, according to the weather reports."

Dismay crept over Alex's delicate features. "I—I must—"

"I know," Oren said. "You have to go. But you *can't*. You go out in this weather, you'll die of exposure within the hour."

Alex tugged at the hem of his borrowed shirt, his mouth drooping. "I am sorry," he whispered. "I do not mean to—"

Oren scooted forward a little on his seat. "Hey," he said gently, and waited until Alex looked up. "I'm glad I can help you."

Alex's mouth worked. "I cannot pay—"

"Not asking for payment," Oren said, waving that off.

"I must go when snow melts," Alex said. "I *must*, Oren."

"Got it," Oren said. "The second the roads are clear, I'll pop you in my jeep and zip you into town."

Alex tilted his head. "Pop?"

"Figure of speech, sorry. I just meant that I understand that time is of the essence, and you have to go as quickly as possible." Oren hesitated. "Do you—is someone waiting for you?"

Alex looked up, tears sheening his eyes. Finally he nodded, jerky and quick, and dropped his gaze back to his knees again.

"Okay then," Oren said, dropping the subject. "I'll take the couch and you can have my bed."

"No," Alex said. "I will take couch."

"It was stuffed by Satan!" Oren protested.

Alex gave him a confused look but shook his head, setting his jaw. "I will sleep here."

"God, you really *are* a donkey," Oren muttered.

"Why do you call me this?" Alex asked.

"Because you're stubborn," Oren said, smiling in spite of himself. "Are you going to fight me on everything?"

"Yes," Alex said, but he was smiling too, lips curving slow and sweet. "Thank you, Oren." His eyes were serious in the dim glow of the banked fire, and Oren rubbed the back of his neck.

"Maybe someday you'll tell me about it," he said, standing up. "Right now, it's time for bed. I'll see you in the morning, okay? Help yourself to anything in the fridge if you get peckish in the night."

He retreated up the stairs to his bedroom, but not even The Importance of Being Earnest was enough to keep his attention, and eventually he dozed off, finger between the pages, thoughts on the stranger in his living room.

When he woke up, he knew immediately that he was alone in the house. He couldn't put his finger on why—a feeling, somehow, a stillness in the air that hadn't been there the night before.

He flung the covers back with a bitten-off curse and scrambled from the bed.

"Alex?"

There was no answer.

Oren swore again and grabbed his coat from the hook by the back door, shoving his boots on and not stopping to lace them properly before plunging out into the bitter cold that stopped his breath in his lungs.

Stupid, stupid kid, he thought, pausing to make sure his jeep was still in the garage. It was, so Alex was on foot, and he'd try to head for town. Oren's house was about two miles outside the city limits, a modest hike on foot for anyone *without* a cracked ankle. Alex was in no shape to be trying to get anywhere by himself right now, even without the weather to contend with.

It was far too icy to drive, so Oren slithered and slid down the hill and broke into a careful jog along the slippery road, hands out to keep his balance, his cheeks stinging and lungs burning with the cold. It was still early, the sun below the trees and the road dark as a result.

Movement caught his eye and he cupped his hands around his mouth. "*Alex!*"

The small shape at the bend in the road spun at that, losing his balance on the ice and disappearing in a wild flailing tumble out of sight.

"*Shit.*" Oren ran faster, praying he didn't fall and break his own ankle, and slithered headlong to a stop at the edge of the ditch, leaning precariously over it. Alex was a crumpled heap in the bottom of the hollow, both hands around his ankle as he rocked back and forth.

Oren half-fell, half-jumped down into the ditch, landing next to Alex with a thud that jarred the wind from him.

"Did you land on your bad foot?" he managed after a minute.

Alex nodded, his face drawn and white with pain.

"Fuck, I'm so sorry," Oren said. "That's my fault. Come on, let's get you out of here. I think your ankle's bad enough that we should try to get you to the hospital."

Alex opened his mouth to say something and snapped it shut as the rumbling of an engine floated through the crisp air.

Oren straightened. ""Who the fuck is *driving* in this? Maybe they can give us a ride."

Alex clutched at him. "*No.*" There was panic on his face and in the desperate strength of his fingers on Oren's coat, and Oren bent to him.

"Hey, easy, it's okay. No one's going to hurt you."

The engine got louder—it sounded like a snowmobile, he realized—and Oren tried to straighten again, to climb out of the ditch and flag down the driver, but Alex was clinging to him with both hands now, on his knees as he tried to keep Oren's head below the road, out of sight. He was clearly well on his way to a full blown panic attack, his skin chalky and eyes huge, breath sharp and short and chest heaving, and Oren abruptly made up his mind.

He dropped to his knees and pulled Alex against his chest, tipping them both sideways until they were lying face to face on the inclined surface of the ditch. The trees arched over them, forming a lacy net high above their heads of bare branches, and the snow was cold and wet, the dirt hard-packed beneath them.

The vehicle was almost on top of them now, and despite the fact that Oren didn't really think they were in any danger, Alex's obvious terror was catching, and Oren found himself holding his breath as it rumbled slowly past.

This close, he could see tiny flecks of gold inside the brown of Alex's eyes. He smelled like damp wool and apples and fear, an acrid tang that scoured the back of Oren's throat when he drew in a deep breath.

Silence fell. Alex was panting in tiny, shallow heaves, his eyes fixed on Oren's face. As Oren watched, a tear slid across the bridge of his nose.

"He will kill you," Alex whispered, and squeezed his eyes shut.

IT WAS several more minutes before Oren was able to get Alex out of the ditch, but finally he cajoled him to his feet. He climbed out first and then reached down and took Alex's hands, pulling him up easily.

But when Alex tried to put weight on his right ankle, he cried out and folded up, hunching into a ball around the pain.

"I… cannot," he managed. "I am sorry, Oren."

Oren touched his shoulder, glancing up and down the road to make sure they were still alone. The sun was coming up, dawn finally beginning to spill over in pale pinks and blues, but it was still hard to see much, where they were.

"Listen," he said. "I'm going to have to carry you, okay?"

Alex looked up at him, clearly reluctant, but finally he nodded.

Oren bent and scooped him up bridal-style, an arm behind Alex's back and the other under his knees, careful of his ankle, and turned for home. It was faster to cut across-country through the snow rather than brave the icy switchback road, so he struck out, his burden almost unnoticeable in his arms.

"So, what would you like for breakfast?" he asked as he walked, mostly to break the awkward silence.

Alex shot him an incredulous look and burst into tears, pressing his face against Oren's chest as his shoulders shook.

Whoops. Oren sped up a little, careful on the treacherous ground and clutching his armload close. It wasn't long before he was climbing the hill behind his house, wading through the snow to the slippery deck and letting them in through the back door.

"Hey, we're here," he said, rubbing Alex's thigh with his thumb as he carried him into the living room. Alex's sobs had tapered off into occasional hiccups, but his face was still buried in Oren's shoulder.

Oren hesitated and then swung right, climbing the stairs to his bedroom and setting Alex down as gently as possible on the bed.

Alex blinked and scrubbed at his face, looking around him. "Oren—"

"Don't argue with me," Oren said. "I'm getting the first aid kit, I'll be right back." He didn't wait for an answer, retreating back down the hall to the bathroom to grab the kit and, as an afterthought, the narcotics.

Alex was sitting with his right leg stretched out in front of him when Oren came back, his chin propped on his left knee as he gazed down at his bad ankle.

"How is it?" Oren asked.

Alex lifted a shoulder. "Am not doctor." The words were clipped but it was obviously pain sharpening his tone.

"Okay, let me look at it," Oren said, sitting down on the end of the bed.

He pulled Alex's tattered boot off over the rapidly swelling ankle and grimaced as he gently felt along the bone.

"I'm not a doctor either," he finally said, looking up. "But I really do think you broke it. I need to take you to the hospital."

Alex shook his head hard. "No."

"Would you rather never walk again?" Oren demanded.

"Is better than *dying*," Alex shot back.

Oren flung his hands up and Alex flinched, pressing his face to his knee again.

"I'm sorry," Oren said instantly, scooting backward to put some space between them. "Alex, would you look at me please?"

There was a heartbeat of silence and then Alex lifted his head, a heartbreaking mixture of fear and defiance in his eyes.

Oren opened his mouth to speak but someone knocked on the door before he could. Alex's eyes shot wide in terror and he covered his mouth with both hands.

"It's okay," Oren said quietly, touching Alex's good knee. "You stay here. Don't make any noise."

Alex reached for him, grabbing Oren's wrist. He was trembling, white as a sheet, and Oren's heart hurt.

"Is him," Alex said raggedly.

"Who?" Oren asked, and then shook his head. No time for that right now. "Never mind. Stay here." He reached out on impulse, cupping Alex's cheek, Alex's eyes wide and terrified above Oren's hand. Then he stood and ran for the door as the knocking came again, louder and more insistent.

THE VISITORS WERE at the front door, not the back door Oren always used, so he had to dash down the stairs two at a time to answer it. He took a second to compose himself with his hand on the doorknob before he swung it open, putting what he hoped was the right blend of surprise and irritation on his face as he gazed up at the two *very* large men on the other side, one of them holding a trash bag.

"Can I help you gentlemen?" Oren said.

The first man, clearly the leader by bearing and build, took a step forward and smiled. He reminded Oren of a leopard, sleek and deadly and handsome, killer claws hidden but there just the same.

"Are you the owner of this house, sir?" he asked. He had a subtle accent, different from Alex's—it sounded eastern European, maybe Russian.

Oren glared at him, bristling. "What tipped you off, the fact that I answered the door?"

The man smiled, baring his teeth. "Of course, I apologize. May we come in?"

Oren set his feet. "No offense, but I'd rather you didn't. I don't know you."

The man tipped his head, smile unwavering. "I understand. My name is Andrei, and I'm looking for a friend of mine. He's a young man, twenty-one years old, off his medication, highly mentally unstable and a danger to himself and others in the state he's in. Have you seen anyone recently, anyone who perhaps appeared unwell?"

Unwell? Oren had to stifle a spike of rage,

praying nothing showed. He pretended to think.

"I'd ask what he looks like, but it doesn't matter—I haven't seen anyone but my own face in the mirror for the past three days. Do you have a business card or anything, so I can call you if he shows up?"

Andrei cocked his head, considering Oren. Finally he smiled. "Of course, sir." He produced a card from his pocket, handing it over with a flourish.

Oren indicated Andrei's companion. "What about him? Does he talk?"

Andrei's smile widened. "When he has to. Thank you for your time, sir." He half-turned as if to go and then stopped, taking the trash bag from his companion and holding it out to Oren. "We found this outside. Did you have an accident, sir?"

"Slipped on the ice yesterday," Oren said airily, mentally kicking himself. Why hadn't he picked it up? He'd forgotten all about that fucking bag, and it must have slid down the hill when he dropped it. "Twisted my ankle, figured I'd pick it up later."

"You're not limping now," Andrei observed. "And there are tracks in the snow around the house. Now, I'm no tracker, but are you sure you haven't had visitors?"

Oren snatched the bag from him. "I heal fast and I went out to check my traps this morning. Is there something else I can help you with?"

"No, I think that's all I need," Andrei said.

He left, his footsteps silent and quick on the ice, and Oren shivered and shut the door, bolting it behind him and running upstairs for the bedroom.

Alex was nowhere to be seen, the bedcovers rumpled, and Oren cursed to himself. "Alex?" he called quietly. "They're gone." He waited, holding his breath, and after a minute, there was a shuffling and Alex emerged from the far side of the bed.

He'd been hiding underneath the bed, Oren realized, and he suddenly wanted to weep. Instead he forced a smile and rounded the bed himself, bending to help Alex up and onto the mattress again.

"Was it… him?" Alex whispered, folding his arms around his knees.

"If by him, you mean Andrei, then yeah," Oren said, sitting down beside him. "It was him and one of his goons. And it's time for *you* to start talking."

Alex looked up sharply. "I cannot," he protested.

"I know you don't want to pull me into this," Oren said, settling himself a little more firmly on the bed, "but I think at this point I'm pretty well… pulled."

Alex's brows drew together but Oren wasn't done.

"You landed on my doorstep, starved and frozen half to death and beaten to a fare-thee-well. You're *terrified* of this Andrei character. I may not have wanted you here, but do you honestly expect me to just let you go, wave goodbye and let you take your chances out there, especially with a broken ankle?"

Alex was trembling, his arms wrapped around himself as if to keep in the terror that wanted to rip him apart, and Oren reached for him without thinking, unable to bear it any longer. He realized what he was doing at the last second and stopped himself, but Alex made a noise in his throat and fell toward him, colliding with Oren's chest and clinging like a desperate bramble.

Oren wrapped his arms around him, gathering Alex up into his lap so that he was securely situated, his face tucked against Oren's throat.

"Okay," Oren whispered, rubbing Alex's back. "Okay. I've got you. Just hold on, donkey. Hold on."

It took several minutes before Alex was composed enough to speak, but finally he stirred and sat up. Oren let him go, shifting his weight so their thighs were pressing together.

"I am from… România," Alex said. "When… I was nineteen, my parents—" He swallowed hard. "Sold… my brother Mihai to the Russians. He was… fifteen."

"*Jesus*," Oren managed. "And you? Did they sell you too?"

Alex shook his head. "I… follow."

Oren thought distantly that he might be sick. "You willingly went into sex slavery to, what? Rescue him?"

"To get him out," Alex said, ducking his

chin and gazing at his lap. "But to find him was long, and I am just one, I am not enough, I cannot—" He took a shaky breath. "So I stay."

"You couldn't get him out by yourself, so you stayed with him," Oren said.

Alex nodded. "We came to America… to here." He drew his good leg back up and pressed his face to it, shoulders drooping.

"How long have you been here?"

"I do not know," Alex said to his knee. "A year?"

Oren shook himself. "Okay, look. I understand why you can't go to the police or the hospital, but why won't you let me give you anything for the pain?"

Alex clutched the bedcovers. When he spoke, his voice was muffled. "With them, I am not…." He hesitated. "What is word? Obey?"

"Obedient," Oren whispered. "You weren't obedient, were you? You fought them."

Alex nodded, closing his eyes and pressing his face to his knee again. "Da. Yes. I fight. So they drug me."

"Okay," Oren said, blinking several times. "So you got out but Mihai didn't?"

Something flickered across Alex's face and he shook his face. "We were… put apart?"

"Separated?" Oren said.

"Da," Alex whispered. "Separated. Mihai did not make it out. Told me… run. So I did." He lifted his head. "I have to go for him, Oren."

"Of course you do," Oren said immediately. "The second the roads are clear, I promise."

Alex's face eased and his shoulders slumped.

Oren patted his thigh. "No more talking right now. Since you won't take anything, it's time for you to sleep. Do you think you can?"

Alex lifted a shoulder noncommittally. "Where… will you be?"

"Close," Oren said. He waited as Alex slid under the covers, biting his lip and white with pain, and then tucked him in, pulling the blankets up and around his shoulders.

Alex reached for him, slim fingers bracketing Oren's wrist.

Oren stopped moving as Alex's thumb moved over his pulse point, brown eyes steady on his face.

"*Mulțumesc*," Alex whispered.

Oren blinked. "I—what?"

"Thank you," Alex said, a smile flickering across his lips. "Thank you, Oren."

Oren took a chance and reached out to smooth the hair off Alex's forehead. "I'll stay where you can hear me," he murmured, and left the room.

3

———

OREN MADE BREAKFAST, gathered a few things from his workshop, and then busied himself cleaning up in the living room and kitchen, but he was jumpy, listening for any noise from the bedroom, and finally his nerves couldn't take it any longer. He sighed, piled food on the breakfast tray, grabbed his book, and climbed the stairs back up.

Alex was on his side, eyes on the door, and he seemed to relax as Oren appeared, the tray in his hands.

"Hungry?" Oren asked.

Alex didn't answer, but he sat up, flinching as the movement dragged at his ankle.

Oren settled the tray across Alex's lap and then sat down on the bed beside him, waiting until Alex met his eyes.

Oren took a deep breath. "I'm not a doctor, but I have to do my best to set your ankle so it doesn't heal crooked, okay? And it's gonna hurt like a bitch when I do. So—" He pulled the bottle of narcotics from his pocket. "I won't force you to take these. If you do, it will be of your own free will, just like every-thing else you do in this house. But I want you to understand that you are *safe*, Alex. You can let yourself relax. You don't have to be in pain right now. I'll watch out for you."

Alex searched his face. "Why?" he asked again.

As before, Oren couldn't figure out how to answer. Finally he lifted a shoulder. "Maybe because I wish someone had done that for me."

Silence fell between them as Alex weighed that.

"What if they come back?" he asked after a minute.

Oren opted for total honesty. "Kid, if they come back, I'm not sure we'll be able to stop them in any case, whether or not you're dopey from taking a narcotic."

Alex studied his face, and then reached out and took the bottle from Oren's hand.

Oren drew a relieved breath. "Just take one," he said, careful to keep his voice normal. "As skinny as you are, we don't want you overdosing."

Alex nodded and tapped one out onto his palm. His hands were shaking, but he swal-lowed it without hesitation, tilting his head back and his throat working, eyes fluttering shut.

Oren waited until Alex opened his eyes

before scooting the tray a little nearer. "I want to wait until it kicks in before I try to immobilize it. In the meantime, I hope you like brown sugar oatmeal," he said. "Demolish that for me, would you?"

Alex tilted his head. "What is… demolish?"

Oren half-laughed. "It means to destroy, to smash or obliterate. Sorry, I keep forgetting to dial it back on the euphemisms." He smacked his forehead as Alex looked even more baffled, and gestured at the oatmeal. "Just… eat that and pretend I'm not here."

He settled in the chair by the window overlooking the valley and the road below, opening his book on his knees as Alex began to eat.

Within twenty minutes, Oren could see the narcotic taking effect. Alex's head drooped, the lines of pain in his face easing and the spoon in his hand wobbling.

Oren put his book down and stood as quietly as possible, tiptoeing to the bed and sliding the spoon from Alex's fingers. He lifted the tray off and set it on the floor beside the bed and turned back, urging Alex down onto his back among the pillows and stuffing one pillow under his bad foot as gently as possible.

"Brace yourself," he said. "I have to palpate the joint and make sure I'm getting it braced as evenly as possible."

Alex took a deep breath and closed his eyes, firming his mouth, and Oren felt along his ankle, pressing delicately along the joint.

Alex twitched a few times but didn't make any noise as Oren lifted his foot and moved it back and forth.

"Sorry, sorry," Oren muttered, not looking up. "Hang in there, I just have to be *sure*—" He picked up the small piece of birch and held it against Alex's ankle. The piece of ash the same length went on the other side, and Oren held them both in place with one hand as he used vet wrap around Alex's calf and ankle until he was satisfied the joint was as straight as possible and immobile.

Then he set his foot down and Alex took a deep, whooping gasp of air and sagged. There were beads of sweat on his face, Oren saw when he looked up.

"I'm done," he said. "You can relax. God, you're a tough one. How are you feeling?"

Alex cracked one eye open and looked at him, and Oren laughed quietly.

"Stupid question, you're right. Think you can rest now?"

Alex nodded and burrowed deep into the pillows, pressing his face into the down and sighing. Oren smoothed the hair off his forehead again.

"You're safe," he said.

He stayed in the bedroom as Alex dozed for the rest of the morning. When he stirred, in the early afternoon, Oren was reading in his chair. He put his book down but didn't move as Alex rolled over, awareness filling his eyes.

"How are you feeling?" Oren asked.

Alex shrugged, a little smile tugging at his mouth. "I am sorry, Oren, but I need to—"

"You need the bathroom, don't you?" Oren jumped up and pulled Alex's covers off, scooping him carefully into his arms. Alex clung to him, a disturbingly light burden, as Oren carried him down the steps to the bathroom.

Back in the bedroom, Oren frowned as he set Alex in the bed.

"What?" Alex asked, out of breath.

"You feel… warm," Oren said. He pushed the curls off Alex's forehead and pressed his palm to the skin. "God, you're burning up."

Alex caught his hand as Oren pulled it away, his eyes full of worry. "No hospital."

"I know," Oren said. "But—"

"No," Alex insisted. "Andrei—will know. And he will kill Mihai, Oren."

Oren sighed.

"*Please*," Alex begged, and sneezed.

"Lie down," Oren said. He sighed again when Alex just stared up at him. "For God's sake, kid, I'm not going to take you to the hospital and risk your brother's life, but don't ask me to be *happy* about it, okay? Now *please* lie down?"

Alex shivered and let go of Oren's wrist, sliding down the bed to curl up in a ball. He accepted the pill that Oren offered him without complaint, swallowing it silently and closing his eyes as Oren pulled the blankets into place.

"Rest," Oren said.

ALEX GOT RAPIDLY WORSE over the course of the afternoon. By the time the sun was down, he was nearly delirious, knees drawn to his chest and tremors wracking his frame, eyes fixed sightlessly on the far wall.

Oren was getting more and more worried. He wasn't a doctor. He had no more medical training than the summer spent as a lifeguard that he'd mentioned to Alex earlier and a brief stint working for a veterinarian, and it in no way qualified him to nurse Alex through what he suspected might well be developing into pneumonia.

Alex needed an actual doctor, antibiotics, someone who could do more than fix a chair or restring a piano.

But it wasn't just a matter of his promise not to bring attention to them—Oren had been telling the truth when he said they couldn't leave. It was still snowing, and the drifts were getting progressively deeper. For better or worse, they were going to have to ride this one out on their own as best they could.

Oren tidied up the mess he'd left and then leaned over Alex's still form. "Hang in there," he whispered.

THE NIGHT PASSED SLOWLY, and Oren dozed fitfully in the chair, waking every time Alex stirred. He didn't get much sleep, but he told himself Alex would be better when the sun came up.

BUT IN THE MORNING, Alex was worse. When Oren woke up, Alex's skin was bone-dry and burning to the touch.

Oren scrambled out of the chair and poured him some water, but Alex didn't rouse to drink it.

"Come on," Oren said, cupping Alex's jaw and tilting the glass. "Please, Alex, wake up, you need to get some fluids in you."

But the water dribbled out the sides of Alex's mouth and his head lolled as Oren set the glass down.

Oren fought back a surge of worry and laid him gently down in the bed, smoothing his hair off his forehead and then running for the bathroom.

He started a lukewarm bath and went back for Alex while the tub filled, gathering him into his arms. Alex didn't wake up, and Oren set his jaw and carried him down the stairs to the bathroom.

He didn't bother taking Alex's clothes off this time. Instead he just set him down directly in the water, cradling his head and making sure it didn't thump against the porcelain.

Oren went to his knees beside the tub, one

hand still behind Alex's head, watching his face.

"Gotta bring that fever down," he whispered.

Alex's eyes moved under their lids as he dreamed.

OREN LOST track of how long they stayed like that. When the water got too cold, he shifted positions carefully, drained the tub and refilled it, making sure Alex's head stayed above the water. His knees were complaining and his back ached, but he didn't move.

Finally, though, Alex stirred. "Oren?" He sounded confused, not that Oren blamed him.

Oren rolled back up to his knees and smiled at him. Alex looked exhausted, the dark circles under his eyes almost blue, his lips white, but his eyes were aware again. Oren felt his forehead and sagged.

"Your fever's broken," he said.

"Why am I in bath, Oren?" Alex asked, plucking his soggy shirt away from his concave chest.

Oren laughed, giddy with relief. "It's a long story but mostly it involves you having a really high fever and me panicking a little bit. How are you feeling?"

"Hungry?" Alex said, ducking his head. "Sorry."

"Why are you sorry?" Oren demanded. "Being hungry is a good thing, it means you're getting better! Can you keep your head above water long enough for me to go get you dry clothes?"

Alex nodded and Oren clambered to his feet and dashed for the bedroom. When he returned, Alex was sitting up in the bathtub, his cheek on his knee. Oren helped him to his feet and onto the bathmat, where he swayed, dripping and pale.

"I'm going to strip you down," Oren said, alarmed, "and then we'll get you dressed as quickly as possible. Okay?"

Alex nodded and Oren set to work, pulling the sodden wool up and over Alex's head and pushing the pants down until he stood bare in front of Oren.

Oren had seen him naked before, of course, five minutes after he first met him, but somehow it was even worse this time. He could count every one of Alex's ribs, span the distance between his jutting hipbones with his spread fingers and thumbs, and even though the worst of the bruising had begun to heal, Oren was suddenly overcome with a fierce need to soothe away the rest of the injuries, until Alex's skin was ivory pale and smooth again, unmarked and whole.

Alex crossed his arms over his chest. "Oren?"

"I'm sorry," Oren said, shaking himself. "Hold onto my shoulder and step into the pants."

There was a small tattoo of a butterfly on Alex's hip, he saw as he gently pulled the sweats into place, blue and green and golden watercolors bleeding into each other in swirling patterns.

Alex was beginning to breathe hard, his complexion whitening even more.

"Almost done," Oren said. He shook out the sweater—one of his favorites, not that he was going to tell Alex that—and eased it over Alex's head.

Then he bent and scooped him up into his arms again. "One deluxe taxi service, coming right up," he said.

"You talk—so strange," Alex said as Oren climbed the stairs back to the bedroom.

Oren laughed and set him down on the bed. "It's been said. Now, you stay there, I'm gonna go get you something to eat, okay?"

He made more oatmeal, listening for any noises from the bedroom, and hurried back as quickly as he could.

Alex was on his side, watching for him, and he pushed himself upright as Oren came through the door.

"It's actually close to dinnertime," Oren said cheerfully, helping Alex situate the pillows behind his back, "but I figured oatmeal would be good. Stick to your ribs and all that."

Alex looked puzzled and a little apprehensive, glancing down at his ribs and then eyeing the oatmeal dubiously. He picked up the spoon without speaking, though, and began to eat as Oren busied himself straightening up the room.

"Have you taken a pill?" he asked when he was done.

Alex shook his head, his shoulders drooping, and Oren sat down on the edge of the bed and touched his knee under the covers.

"Can you rest awhile now?"

Alex nodded and then reached for Oren's wrist as he made to stand. "Will you… stay?"

Oren sank back to the bed and Alex visibly relaxed. Oren looked a little closer. "It's okay, you know," he said.

Alex hunched his shoulders. "They will… come back," he finally said, his voice almost inaudible.

"Maybe," Oren said. "I got rid of them once, I can do it again. I'm a pretty fast talker. You're safe here."

Alex stared at his lap. "Nowhere is safe," he whispered.

Oren stood up, taking the tray off Alex's legs and setting it on the floor beside the bed. "Will you scoot down?" he said, making a motion with his hand, and Alex slid down the mattress onto his side. Oren waited until he was still before he climbed onto the bed behind him. He didn't touch him, just lay quietly, a foot of room between them, and waited.

Alex caught his breath, every muscle going tense as Oren got comfortable. When he didn't move again, though, he began to relax, the tautness of his body draining away, and wriggled backward a few inches again, until they were almost touching.

"Tell me about Mihai," Oren murmured.

He could hear the smile in Alex's voice when he answered. "Mihai… is so smart. Much smarter than me. He is going to be doctor. Or—ortho—"

"Orthopedist?" Oren said.

"Da. Yes," Alex said. He wriggled back, a little closer to Oren's body heat. "He taught himself English. He was… taught me—no. He was teach?"

"Teaching?" Oren suggested.

"Yes," Alex said. "He was teaching me. My English not good. His much better, you will see."

"What does he look like?"

"His hair is—" Alex lapsed into his own language and Oren blinked at the unfamiliar phrase as Alex twisted to see his face. "Your hair is what color?"

"Dark brown," Oren said.

"Dark brown," Alex repeated. "Mine?" He tugged at a lock of his hair and Oren couldn't help his smile.

"Yours is blond."

Alex smiled back at him. "Mihai's hair is… middle?"

"Between dark brown and blond?" Oren said.

Alex nodded. "His eyes…." He glanced around as if for inspiration and his gaze caught on the sleeve of the sweater he was wearing, dark green, soft and densely knit. He lifted his arm. "What color is this?"

"Green," Oren said quietly, unable to take

his eyes off Alex's face. His color was coming back, a little animation returning, and his hair tumbled over his high forehead, obscuring the cut on his temple.

Alex smiled brilliantly at him and turned back over, curling up against Oren's body again. "Green," he repeated. "Mihai's eyes are green."

Oren touched his hip, Alex relaxed and trusting now, his long limbs loose and easy in their sprawl across the bedspread.

"I can't wait to meet him," Oren murmured. "We'll figure out how to get him back once the ice melts."

"Can I have pill, Oren?" Alex asked, his voice hesitating.

"Of course," Oren said instantly. He managed to find the bottle without sitting up and shook a pill out onto Alex's palm.

"You are… good man," Alex said quietly after he'd swallowed it.

He fell asleep eventually as Oren lay beside him and the sun went down, shadows lengthening across the floor and merging into velvety black around them.

4

———————

THEY WOKE up early the next morning, the sun sending questing rays of light through the window to break through the gloom. Oren sat up and yawned, then stood and turned to pick Alex up, who lifted his arms to be carried.

When they were done in the bathroom, Alex made an inarticulate noise of protest when Oren made to take him back to the bedroom.

Oren hesitated on the stairs. "What is it?"

Alex fidgeted, hands in his lap. "I want… will you be with me?"

"I was thinking of working in my shop today, actually," Oren said. "I've got orders I need to fill."

"Oh… alright." Alex looked down at his hands, twisted together so tightly the whites of his knuckles showed.

"Hey," Oren said gently. "Can you talk to me? What is it?"

Alex looked up at him, eyes dark with shame. "I do not… want to be alone, Oren."

Oren's breath caught. "Of course you don't. Okay. How about I put you on the couch for now, while I make breakfast, and then I'll make you a comfortable throne downstairs where you can watch me while I work?"

Alex ducked his head, relief filling his expressive face. "Thank you," he whispered.

Oren made pancakes on his favorite griddle as Alex watched from a chair at the tiny dining room table.

"The secret," he explained as he flipped the first one, "is to beat the eggs until they're frothy and then add some vanilla. You'll have people begging you for your recipe, I promise."

Alex's lips curved. He looked fascinated. "You were cook, maybe? Before…." He waved a hand. "This? Or were you always this?"

Oren tensed. "I—no. I wasn't a chef." He slid the pancake onto a plate and poured the batter for the next as stillness fell between them.

Alex's face was clouded. "I am sorry, Oren," he said unhappily. "I did not mean to —" He made a frustrated motion. "I do not know word."

Oren set the spatula down and crossed the small kitchen to stand in front of Alex's chair as Alex gazed up at him, his mouth drooping.

"Pry," Oren said. "You didn't mean to pry."

Alex nodded, lowering his eyes.

"I wasn't always… this," Oren said.

Alex looked up at him through his lashes and Oren wanted suddenly, desperately, to kiss him, to sink his fingers into Alex's soft curls and taste his mouth.

He cleared his throat and turned back to the stove before the pancake could burn. "In a previous life, I was a line-cook in a circus," he said over his shoulder.

"Really?" Alex said.

"Shit you not," Oren said, holding up three fingers. He glanced back to see Alex looking confused yet again, and Oren groaned. "I mean… yeah, really. It was only for one summer, and it was some of the hottest, most miserable work I've ever done, but boy, can I break down a big top faster than anyone else you know." He stopped to consider. "Probably."

Alex was smiling as Oren set the pancakes in front of him. "What is big top?"

"It's the tent for the circus, where the main acts are held," Oren said. "Try those, tell me what you think."

THEY ATE TOGETHER at the small table, Oren watching the way Alex applied himself to his food. He ate neatly, as if he'd been taught manners, but he hunched forward, elbows out, and chewed and swallowed rapidly, as if braced to have the plate yanked away from him at any moment.

He wanted to kill Andrei slowly, Oren decided as Alex finished his pancakes and mopped up the last of the syrup.

"Good?" he said.

Alex nodded, his mouth full, and Oren smiled at him as he cleared the table.

The breakfast mess put away, Oren carried Alex downstairs to his workshop and settled him in the overstuffed recliner that usually gathered dust and piles of unread mail, making a nest of blankets and pillows and fussing until he was sure Alex was comfortably situated.

"Good?" he said, standing back with hands on his hips. "I need to work on one of my tree houses. Are you okay where you are? Would you like me to find you somewhere more comfortable? Maybe I should bring a better chair downstairs for you."

Alex was laughing. "You fuss like an old *mătușă*," he said. "I am okay. I like watch—to watch?"

"You'll tell me when you get tired?"

"Da," Alex said.

Oren settled in at his bench and picked up a piece of driftwood as Alex shifted so he could see a little better.

"What do you make?" Alex asked. He hunched his shoulders as Oren looked up. "I am sorry—"

"No, it's fine," Oren said hastily. "You can

talk all you want, it won't bother me a bit. I like the sound of your voice."

I like your smile, too, he thought as it bloomed across Alex's face.

He cleared his throat. "I make and sell miniature tree houses that look like they've grown organically in the wood branches that I've chosen for them. They're pretty popular, so I make a nice amount of money for them, and I have an agreement with a place in town to sell them for me, so I don't have to worry about a storefront or overhead or employees or anything like that. All I have to do is make them, which is what I'm good at." He was busy with the branch in front of him as he spoke, stripping it of leaves and twigs, paring it down to what he'd need to add the foundation for the tiny house with the curving pathway up the trunk of the branch.

"On weekends," he continued, "I sometimes go antiquing." He glanced up in time to catch Alex's baffled expression, and laughed. "Americans in general must be so confusing to you. I'm sorry."

"Yes," Alex agreed, lips curving.

"I go to estate sales, flea markets, that sort of thing," Oren said, "and I buy interesting old pieces of furniture, things that I can fix up and sell for a profit. Sometimes I do it for commissions—I usually have a list of things that clients are looking for at any given time, and sometimes I just buy something because I like the look of it and I think I might be able to do something with it. Like the piano over there, for instance." He jerked his head toward the corner.

Alex sat upright so quickly he nearly over-balanced. "You have piano?"

"Do you play?" Oren asked, startled.

Alex nodded, his eyes bright, his fingers flexing in his lap as if touching invisible keys. "Can I—"

"It's due for a tune up," Oren said, but he picked Alex up and carried him to the piano bench. Alex's body was tense in his arms, straining toward the instrument, and he folded back the lid with reverent hands, smoothing his fingers across the ivories as Oren sat down next to him on the bench.

Oren had the distinct feeling that he'd ceased to exist as Alex settled his hands in place and began to play.

The melody rolled out, a haunting Brahms lullaby, and Alex's eyes closed as his fingers danced across the keys, coaxing the music out.

Oren found himself holding his breath, watching him bringing song to sweet, vibrant life, working his way through the descant in rippling waves, his fingers unerringly finding their place.

When the song ended, Alex dropped his hands into his lap. There were tears on his cheeks, Oren saw with a jolt.

Alex turned his head and met Oren's eyes, his lips parting, soft and wet. He swayed a little closer, his lashes sweeping down.

Oren took a deep breath. "That was lovely," he murmured. "Did you play for Mihai a lot?"

Alex straightened, his face clearing. "I—yes. That was… his favorite song. It helps him sleep."

"Where did you learn?" Oren asked, standing up and returning to his workstation as Alex began to play another tune, a quick and lilting refrain.

"The priest in our village," Alex said over the music. "He was also… schoolteacher. He teach—" He made a frustrated noise and changed keys. "*Taught*. He taught us. I did—more things for him. Cleaned blackboards, swept floors, washed windows, and he taught—" He flashed Oren a triumphant smile, the music never stopping. "He taught me to play."

"You're very good," Oren said as he picked up the branch. "What other pieces did he teach you?"

Alex shrugged and began a complicated glissando, fingers a blur across the keys. "I do not always know the music? I just… play."

Oren watched him, awed. "God, you're a fucking savant. You should be performing at Carnegie Hall, not my dusty workshop."

"What is Carnegie Hall?" Alex asked, segueing into a slower piece. His brown eyes looked more peaceful than Oren had seen them yet, the lines of fear and worry in his face easing and an almost-smile on his full lips.

"It's a place where really talented people go

to perform," Oren said. "One day you should go there, you and Mihai."

Alex did smile at that, his eyes dreamy. "I would like that."

He played for a while longer as Oren went back to work, but after about an hour, he fumbled a note and Oren looked up sharply from the tiny staircase in his hands. Alex's head was drooping over the keys, his long body a curve of exhaustion.

"Shit, I'm sorry," Oren said, putting down his tools. "Are you sure you wouldn't rather just go to bed?"

Alex shook his head and allowed Oren to help him upright and over to the comfortable seat he'd made for him, sinking into it with a stifled groan. "Please, I want to stay with you," he said, his long fingers soft and supplicating on Oren's sleeve.

Oren ruthlessly squashed the butterfly that stirred in his chest. "Alright," he warned. "But it's going to be pretty boring."

"I will… sleep, maybe," Alex said through a yawn, and curled into a ball that belied his height, pillowing his head on his arms.

Oren smiled down at him and pulled the blankets up over his shoulders. "Let me know if you need anything."

"The snow to melt," Alex said.

Oren huffed a laugh and felt Alex's forehead. It was still warmer than he liked, but at least he wasn't running the blazing fever from earlier. "When I gain control of the weather, you'll be the first to know."

BUT INSTEAD, the snow started falling harder. Oren watched, progressively more troubled, as the sky darkened outside his window and fat white flakes bumped and swirled soundlessly against the panes of glass, gathering along the sill as Alex slept.

Oren tiptoed up the steps and pulled out his little wireless radio, tuning it to an AM station that broadcast nothing but weather reports. Sure enough, Cheyenne was getting hammered and it wasn't letting up any time soon. Temperatures were expected to be well below zero for the next week, the pleasant robotic voice informed him, and residents were advised to stay inside except in cases of severe emergency.

Alex was going to lose his mind, Oren thought, chewing on his lip. Another week before they could even *begin* to look for Mihai?

Oren stepped into his boots and headed outside to grab some wood off the pile. When he came back in, shivering convulsively, he heard Alex's voice raised in alarm from downstairs.

"Oren? *Oren!*"

"I'm here!" Oren said. He nearly twisted his own ankle galloping down the stairs to where Alex was struggling out of his nest of blankets, terror on his face. He reached for him and Oren gathered him up without thinking, pulling him close. Alex was trembling, Oren realized with a rush of guilt. "Hey, easy," he murmured. "I just went to get more wood for the fire, I didn't mean to scare you."

Alex pushed his face into Oren's collarbone, clinging to his neck. "I dreamed—" he said, his voice muffled. "Dreamed you were dead, that—that Mihai was…." He choked on a sob and tightened his grip.

"I'm right here," Oren repeated, stroking his hair. "I'm fine, see? And we're going to get Mihai back, you just have to trust me."

"*When?*" Alex burst out, pushing away. He pointed at the window, anguish on his face. "Is snowing *more*, Oren, how will I do this?"

Oren sat down beside him on the edge of the chair, still holding Alex's hands. "I want you to listen to me. Andrei thinks you're dead right now, yes?"

Alex lifted a shoulder, tears on his face. "I do not know."

"Odds are good," Oren said, rubbing Alex's knuckles, arches of bone prominent beneath his thumb. "Once the snowstorm's blown over, he'll probably send men out to look for your body. But until then, we have a little breathing room."

"I do not know what you *mean*," Alex said, frustration ringing in his voice as he pulled his hand away.

Oren gently recaptured it. "I mean that Mihai is safe where he is. Andrei won't do anything to him because he thinks you're dead. So why would Mihai be in danger? Andrei can't use him against you because as far as he knows, you died in the first snowfall after your escape."

Alex's face cleared. "Oh… I see. He is still… whore, though."

Oren winced. "I know. And I hate that, I wish I could fix it right now, but I can't, and Andrei's not going to let him get hurt, not when Mihai can earn him money. Does that make sense?"

"*Da*," Alex said. He leaned forward, letting his forehead drop to Oren's shoulder. "How long, Oren?"

"A week," Oren said, grimacing.

Alex just sighed though. "*Bine*," he whispered. "A week. Then I go. Can I… have pill, Oren?"

Oren cupped the back of his head, feeling the delicate bumps of his skull. "I'll do you one better. How about a pill and dinner by the fireplace? We can talk about our favorite movies and you can tell me who your celebrity crush is. Mine is Mark Hamill from A New Hope. God, he was such a twink."

Alex lifted his head, a furrow appearing between his brows. "You are… such a strange man, Oren."

Oren laughed out loud and stood up as Alex lifted his arms to be picked up. "I came to terms with that a long time ago. We need to eat the rest of my bread before it goes stale, so how do you feel about grilled cheese sandwiches?"

"I have never had one," Alex confessed.

Oren gasped and began climbing the

steps. "Well, hang onto your britches, kid, because you're in for a treat."

Alex sighed and put his head down on Oren's shoulder, clearly defeated, and Oren laughed again.

5

———

ALEX WAS DELIGHTED with the grilled cheese sandwich and ate two and a half before he slowed down, grimacing and rubbing his stomach as he leaned back against the couch's lumpy cushions.

"Ate too much?" Oren said. He was sitting cross-legged beside the fire, working on a carving that he wanted to put in one of his houses.

Alex ducked his head. "I will finish it," he said. "I did not mean to waste—"

"Hey, no!" Oren said, looking up. "I made that food for you. And I can always wrap it up and stick it out in the snow if you want to save it for later."

Alex's brows drew together. "The... snow?"

Oren winked at him and blew the shavings off the piece of wood in his hands. "Nature's freezer. Who needs electricity?"

Alex's face cleared. "Ah, I see."

Companionable silence fell as Oren whittled around a knot in the pine.

"What do you make?" Alex asked after a minute.

"I'm not sure yet," Oren confessed, turning the wood to inspect the other side.

Alex looked baffled when Oren glanced up. "But… how do you know… where to put knife then?"

"It tells me," Oren said, smiling at his own whimsy. "Or more accurately, it *shows* me what it wants to be. I carve in tiny bits and I let it take the shape that it's supposed to take."

"The knife knows where to go," Alex said, nodding. His eyelids were drooping, the narcotic taking effect, and Oren set his carving aside and stood up.

"I think it's bedtime."

Alex's head lolled as Oren scooped him up and he turned his face into Oren's chest with a sigh, wrapping Oren's sweater around two fingers and hanging on.

Oren settled his armload and climbed the stairs to the bedroom. Alex was already asleep when Oren put him down in the bed, his face soft and mouth lax. The butterfly stirred again in Oren's chest, stretching its wings.

No. Oren set his jaw and pulled the blankets up over Alex's shoulders, tucking them into place and then tiptoeing back out of the room.

HE READ on the couch in the flickering twilight until he dozed off, and finally curled up on his side, finding a place that was halfway comfortable among the lumpy cushions and drifting back to sleep.

He dreamed of fire and blood and a young boy screaming Alex's name and woke with a start, the weak morning sun slanting across his face.

There was no sound from his room, but when he climbed the stairs, Alex was out of bed and halfway to the door, his face white and set with pain as he braced himself on the wall and hopped on his good foot.

"Goddammit, Alex," Oren said, lunging for him and pulling his arm around his neck. "I'm here to *help* you."

Alex flinched when Oren reached for him but then relaxed, sinking against him with a grateful sigh and letting Oren take his weight.

"I thought you were… sleeps," he said, his teeth clenched. "Slept?"

"Asleep or sleeping, either would work," Oren said as they reached the top of the stairs. He hesitated. "It'll hurt to hop down the stairs. Will you let me carry you?"

Alex was swaying, sweat on his forehead, and he clenched his jaw but nodded.

Oren put his arm behind Alex's legs and swept him off his feet. Alex squeaked, startled, but Oren just winked at him and jogged down the steps to the bathroom.

He leaned against the wall, back turned to give Alex his privacy, and waited for him to get done. "So do you want to hang out in the workshop with me again today? I've got a bunch of orders that I'm behind on, really need to catch up on things."

Alex flushed the toilet and hopped to the sink to wash his hands. "I will not be in your way?"

"Not at all," Oren said. "I do have to gather some more wood first—we're getting low. Will you be okay on the couch until I come back?"

Alex nodded and Oren scooped him up gently to carry him out of the bathroom, careful of his ankle.

"Feels like you're gaining a little weight," Oren said as he took him down the stairs and put him on the couch. "Guess you like my cooking, huh?"

Alex ducked his head. "It is… not bad. I suppose it will do."

Oren stared at him for a minute and then he saw the smile on Alex's face. "You sassy little *shit!*" he said, starting to laugh. "You think you can do better, you go right ahead and try!"

Alex was grinning, dimples flashing in his cheeks, and the butterfly in Oren's chest spread its wings wide. He caught his breath and sobered.

"I'll be right outside the back door, you need me, just holler, okay?"

Alex nodded and Oren tugged his coat on, stepping into his snow boots before braving the outdoors.

The cold bit into him, sinking its sharp teeth deep, and he dragged his gloves from his pocket with a gasp. "Fucking hell, *why* did I choose this state? I couldn't have picked Hawaii?"

The snow was falling hard and fast, gathering on his eyelashes and melting on his lips as he staggered toward the small shed beside the dumpster and hauled the door open, knocking several icicles off in the process.

He gathered an armful of wood that he'd chopped earlier that summer and stumbled the short distance back to the house, nearly tripping over the door jamb as he shoved the door open and burst inside.

"It's cold enough to freeze the balls off a brass monkey!" he said as he kicked the door shut and stomped the snow from his boots.

Alex looked confounded. "Why would a brass monkey have balls?"

"Who the fuck knows why a brass monkey does anything?" Oren said, grinning at him, and dropped the wood on the pile by the fireplace.

Alex's face cleared. "I see. In my country, we say *e frig de crapă pietrele.*"

"You what now?"

Alex huffed an amused breath. "So cold the stones crack."

Oren straightened, putting his fists in the small of his back and stretching the kinks out with a groan. "I like that. Come on, you, let's go have breakfast."

He took off his jacket but Alex shook his

head when Oren reached for him and struggled to his feet on his own.

"Can walk," he said.

Oren stared at him. "You're kidding me right now."

Alex set his jaw. "Is not so bad. See?" He made a tentative hop, balancing himself on the back of the couch, and Oren resisted the urge to cover his face.

"What's the Romanian word for donkey?"

Alex glanced at him. "*Măgar*. Why?"

"I'm gonna start calling you that," Oren said. He stepped up beside Alex, not touching him. "You're possibly the most stubborn person I've ever *met*."

Alex's lips twitched. "Ah. In that case, *catâr* is word you want." He hesitated at the top of the stairs, looking stymied, and Oren sighed.

"Will you at least let me help you down the stairs, *catâr*?"

Alex's smile was breathtaking, spreading across his face slowly and lighting up his brown eyes. "Yes, Oren."

Oren's sigh of relief was exaggerated but worth it for the laugh he got from Alex, and he slipped his arm around Alex's narrow waist and took most of his weight as they went down the stairs.

At the table, he settled Alex in the chair and turned to his pantry. "First thing on my list today—make you a crutch and a proper cast for your ankle."

"You can *make* me these things?" Alex asked.

Oren backed out of his pantry with the containers of flour and sugar in his hands. "Kid, you'd be amazed at the things I could make if I put my mind to it. Built this house, didn't I?"

Alex glanced around the kitchen, his eyes widening. "You *built* this house?"

Oren grinned as he set the containers on the counter. "I know, you wouldn't think it to look at me, but I am pretty handy with these." He held up his hands and wriggled his fingers. "Get it? *Handy?*"

Alex laughed, ducking his head. "You are… ridiculous. How long—did house take?"

Oren began measuring ingredients as he thought. "Two—no, three years, I think. I bought the land for a song because I knew the guy selling it and then it was just a matter of building it as I could afford it."

"You… sing for the land?" Alex said, his brows scrunched together, and Oren had to put the flour down as he laughed.

"I'm sorry," he managed when he finally sobered. "I keep forgetting how literal you are. No, I didn't sing for the land. It's just another expression—it means I got it for a really good price."

"And then you build all this—" Alex gestured at the kitchen, the staircase and banister down to the workshop, words clearly failing him. "By *yourself?*"

Oren shrugged. "I mean, I got a stonemason to pour the foundation. Had an electrician do the basic wiring, because I'm not good with that kind of thing. Everything else, though… yeah. It was all me." He held up a finger in a *wait* gesture and kicked aside the rug on the floor in front of the sink. Alex followed his movements as Oren knelt, running his hands along the seams of the boards, and jumped when he thumped one with his fist.

On the other side of the kitchen, a trapdoor rose silently on oiled hinges, and Alex's mouth fell open.

Oren couldn't help his grin. "I mostly keep tax documents and other boring stuff in there, but yeah."

Alex looked at him silently, awe in his eyes, and Oren stomped ruthlessly on the butterfly in his chest. *He's not for you.*

"Really not that big a deal," he said lightly, turning to the griddle and lighting the burner. "So I'll see if I've got some wood that'll work for crutches. I think I've got at least one that's long enough, and I can go out and look for another one later, once it stops snowing."

THEY ATE TOGETHER, Oren watching Alex's hands as he cut his pancakes into neat squares and ate them in rapid bites, one-two and then again until his plate was clean.

When he was done, he looked up and Oren felt like a voyeur caught peeping in a window, but Alex was smiling at him, crossing his knife and fork on the plate.

"I like your pancakes," he said. "Thank you."

"Sure thing," Oren said. He cleared his throat. "So I'll wash up here and then are you going to let me carry you down to the workshop or are you going to be a *catâr* again?"

Alex laughed out loud, a sound of pure delight, and Oren wanted to kiss the laughter off his mouth, taste his smile and trace the line of his jaw, but he just sucked in air and stood to begin stacking dishes.

You've been alone too long, he told himself as he cleaned the kitchen. *Stupid, to think it could last.*

DOWN IN HIS WORKSHOP, Oren got busy shaping and turning the wood for Alex's cast on his lathe as Alex watched the process, clearly fascinated. It took a while, and a lot of measuring of Alex's ankle and foot, referencing the pictures of casts in an old encyclopedia set he had on his bookshelf and making sure that everything lined up, but finally he snapped the last piece into place.

Alex sagged. "*Oh.*"

"Okay?" Oren asked, worried.

Alex smiled at him. "Yes," he said simply. "Much better. Thank you, Oren."

Next up was the crutch. Alex watched, clearly absorbed, as Oren rooted through his

saved wood, muttering to himself and occasionally holding up a piece to see if it was long
enough.

"Why'd you have to be so *tall*, anyway?"
he sighed after the fourth piece proved too
short, and was delighted to see Alex smile.

"Perhaps I should get on knees," Alex
suggested. "Be short like you."

Oren gasped in mock outrage and Alex's
laugh pealed out again. *Oh help*, Oren
thought despairingly.

Finally, he came up with a section of oak
that proved long enough and he set to work
smoothing it down and sanding it in prepara-
tion for the arm piece.

"Do you want to play the piano?" he
asked without looking up.

"*Yes*," Alex said, so quickly that Oren
knew he'd been waiting to be asked, but he
waved away help when Oren offered it and
hopped to the bench himself.

THEY SPENT the morning that way, Alex only
stopping his playing when Oren needed to
measure the crutch against him and make sure
it was the right length, and eventually Oren
declared it to be lunch time.

"Is crutch ready?" Alex asked.

Oren rubbed his chin. "I'm not happy
with it," he admitted. "I think it could be a lot
better and I don't have a rubber tip to keep it

from sliding all over the place so you'll have to be careful, but yeah, give it a whirl."

He held it out and Alex tucked it under his arm and took a careful step. He made his way around the workshop, avoiding the obstacles with his lower lip caught between his teeth and a furrow between his brows and then looked up, his smile blinding.

"Is *good*, Oren. I can walk!"

"Yeah?" Oren grinned back at him. "You're gonna insist on walking up the stairs, aren't you?"

"Yes," Alex said, his smile widening.

Oren sighed loudly just to hear him laugh again.

On the stairs, Oren touched Alex's arm. "Look," he said, and drew aside one of the heavy wall-coverings to reveal a small door just big enough for a medium-sized person to fit through on hands and knees.

"What is it?" Alex asked.

Oren opened the door in answer, and cold air swept over them, making them shiver. "It's… well, if you need to get out fast, this dumps you out on the hillside just above the road."

Alex looked at him, eyes considering. "Why would you need this thing, Oren?"

Oren flinched and shut the door, locking it quickly. "It was fun," he said, and motioned for Alex to continue up the stairs. "I liked putting in secrets only I knew about."

HALFWAY THROUGH LUNCH, Alex's body began drooping and he stifled a yawn with the back of his hand, looking up guiltily. "Sorry," he said.

"For what?" Oren said. "Being beat all to hell last week and still recovering? Catching pneumonia? Or just being generally starved and malnourished and exhausted?"

Alex's shoulders rounded and he dropped his hands into his lap. "I do not—"

Oren took a breath, forcing back the protective fury. "None of what happened to you is your fault," he said around the lump in his throat. "You never have to apologize to me. You've done *nothing* wrong."

Alex looked up, mouth working, but nothing came out, and Oren stood.

"I think you should rest," he said. "Will you let me take you to the bedroom?"

Alex swallowed and then nodded, and Oren picked him up.

Upstairs in the bedroom, he put him down on the bed and Alex caught his wrist as Oren stood.

"Do you—" Alex faltered and then seemed to find his courage, looking up into Oren's eyes. "Do you want to fuck, Oren?"

Oren flinched. "What—"

"I see... how you look at me," Alex continued. "I have not money to repay you, but I can—"

"*No.*" Oren jerked away, stumbling backward, and fled.

He BOLTED from the house and ran for the cover of the forest, startling a flock of birds from their rest, their wings thunderous as they exploded into the air.

Oren wove through the trees, heading for his favorite spot, the massive bur oak he'd camped under when he'd been building his house. There was peace to be had here, whether it was sleeping in its branches or slinging a hammock beneath it or simply lying on the ground, cradled in its roots and gazing up at the stars through its canopy during warm summer nights.

The cold stung his face as Oren burst into the clearing, forging his way through the snow that came up to his thighs to reach the oak's trunk. He leaned forward, putting his bare hands on the bark, and took a shaky breath.

"What am I supposed to do?" he said, and even to himself he sounded like a child, lost and frightened. "He needs more than I can give him. He needs *help*, not me."

The oak offered up no answers and Oren closed his eyes and rested his forehead against its frozen surface, shivering. "Not me," he whispered.

When he got back to the house, he couldn't open the door. His hands were numb, white with cold, and his fingers refused to bend properly.

Oren swore under his breath and tried again but his hands slid off the cold brass of the doorknob and the door stayed stubbornly closed.

Fucking idiot, he told himself, and tucked his hands into his armpits to warm them up, but just then the door swung open and Alex was revealed in the doorway.

"Oren," he said.

"Uh… hey," Oren said awkwardly. "Thanks."

Alex hopped sideways to let Oren inside. "You must get warm."

"Yeah," Oren said as he shuffled into the house. "I'm… yeah. Okay."

Alex must have stoked the fire while Oren was gone, because it was crackling merrily in the stone fire pit he'd laid himself. It had taken him several weeks, and he still stubbed his toe on that one stone that stuck out at an awkward angle, but it was one of the first things he'd built in the house and he couldn't help being proud of it.

He knelt in front of the fire, holding out his hands and hissing as the heat hit his skin, his nerves lighting up in agonized protest at being revived.

"F-fuck," he muttered, shifting his weight. "I've done some stupid shit, but that takes the cake."

Alex wrapped a blanket around his shoulders, making Oren jump, and then settled himself on the cobblestones beside him, gazing at the flames.

Oren huddled inside the blanket, soaking up the heat of the fire, and silence fell between them.

"You were coming to look for me," he said suddenly, and it was Alex's turn to jump. "Oh my god," Oren continued, facing him, "you thought I was freezing to death in the snow and you were coming out to find me."

Alex lifted a shoulder, his mouth twisting like he tasted something bitter. "Is my fault."

"*No*," Oren said. He ached to touch him, but instead he clutched the blanket closer to his chest. "Alex, I—" He fell silent. "It's not your fault," he finished lamely.

Alex's silence said clearly that he didn't believe him but he didn't feel like arguing.

Oren sighed. "I'm not... I'm not good at this shit. Talking about stuff."

Alex's eyebrow went up. "*You*, not good at talking?"

"Shut up," Oren said, bumping him with his shoulder, and just like that, the awkwardness began to ease between them. Alex swayed into the contact with Oren's side, smiling a little, and Oren didn't even think about it before he opened the blanket and wrapped it around Alex, pulling him into the circle of his arms.

Alex sagged against him with a choked noise, trembling and pressing his fist to his mouth. "I am so sorry," he whispered into Oren's chest. "So sorry, Oren, I—"

"You still have nothing to apologize for," Oren managed. "Just… no sex, okay?"

Alex nodded. "Okay."

The fire popped and crackled as a piece of kindling shifted. Just as Oren was sure Alex was asleep, though, he stirred.

"I want to show you something," he said.

Oren let him go so he could sit up, and Alex dug in the pocket of the sweatpants that Oren had given him, pulling out the piece of paper he'd had on him when Oren had found him.

Alex held it out and Oren took it, unfolding it. It was a photograph, taken on black and white film, of two boys standing in a creek, wet to their waists. Even with his sharp angles softened by childhood, Alex was immediately recognizable, laughing up at the camera with his arm slung around a younger boy.

Mihai wasn't looking at the camera. He was looking at Alex, adoration in his eyes, a streak of mud on his cheek and his hair standing on end.

"Oh, Alex," Oren whispered.

Alex touched the edge of the photograph with one slender finger. "I am… all he has," he husked. "He needs me."

Oren gave him the picture back and waited for Alex to carefully stow it away in his pocket before pulling him into his arms again.

"Soon," he murmured. "I promise."

Alex nodded, his hair brushing Oren's chin. Silence fell once more and slowly Alex slid down until he was draped half across Oren's lap, long limbs relaxed in sleep, his face soft in the flickering firelight.

Oren wriggled a little, getting comfortable, and pulled out the piece of wood he'd been whittling on and his carving knife. He thought he knew now what it wanted to become.

6

OREN CARRIED Alex to bed when he couldn't force his eyes to stay open any longer, and went back downstairs to the couch to sleep himself, wriggling and muttering to himself as he tried to get comfortable in its lumpy embrace.

THE NEXT DAY, he took stock of his pantry with a drooping sense of dismay. Alex, sitting at the kitchen table, looked worried as Oren backed out and turned to face him.

"Nothing for it," Oren said, forcing a smile. "I'm gonna have to go hunting."

Alex stiffened. "Oren—"

"I wouldn't if I thought we could make it," Oren said, scratching the back of his neck. "But we have no source of protein, we ate the last of my eggs earlier, all I have now are dry goods and a little milk about to clabber."

"I do not need much," Alex said, clutching at the fabric of his pants. "I will—I will eat small."

"Absolutely not," Oren said. "The radio said this could go on for another forty-eight hours, and you need proper food. You're recovering from an illness and healing God knows how many broken bones. I *have* to go, Alex."

Alex's mouth wobbled.

"You'll be fine," Oren said gently before he could speak. "Look. You've got your crutch, right? You can get to the bathroom and back to the bed or the couch. You can read, or nap, or whatever you feel like doing. There are a few pancakes left over from last time, I saved them. You can eat those while I'm gone. Maybe don't try to cook unless you know how to use a wood stove though. I don't know how long it'll take, but—"

"What if—"

"They won't come back," Oren said. "If they do, you can—" He turned in a circle for inspiration and a thought occurred to him. "Come upstairs with me a minute."

It took more than a minute, Alex insisting on using his crutch and not being helped, but they made it to the bedroom, where Oren pulled open the doors to the wardrobe he'd built into the side of the hill, nestling it right into the rock.

"Look," he said. He took Alex's wrist and

showed him how to find the switch, hidden at the back of the wardrobe behind the clothes hanging there. They pressed it together and the floor of the wardrobe slid back into the rock silently. "It's a false bottom," Oren said as Alex's eyes widened. "More than big enough to hold you. If they come back, you get in there and wait for me. There's a release button from the inside if you need to get out on your own."

Alex's eyes were panicky but he took a ragged breath in through his nose and nodded.

Oren smiled at him. "Go on back downstairs if you think you can make it. I won't be long."

He got dressed in his winter gear as quickly as he could and went back out to the living room to find Alex on the couch, curled in a ball with his arms around his knees, watching for him anxiously.

Oren spread his arms, nylon rustling. "I clean up pretty nice, right?"

When that failed to get a smile, Oren sighed and tucked his heavy gloves into his belt. "I'll be as quick as I can," he said gently.

Alex pressed his face into his knees and didn't answer. Oren hesitated, but finally headed for the garage and his snowshoes. Back in the house, he retrieved his rifle from its case, loaded it, and checked his pack for the second time, acutely aware of Alex's still form on the couch.

Finally ready, he stood and slung his pack

onto his shoulders. Alex stayed where he was, no longer seeming panicked so much as hopeless, his eyes dull as he watched Oren.

Oren cleared his throat. "I, um. I'll be back." He headed for the door, listening for Alex, but there was silence behind him, and Oren firmed his mouth and stepped outside.

He got the snowshoes strapped on and glided over the snow up the hill behind his house, covering ground quickly. The air was cold and sharp as blades, slicing his lungs as he made his way along, and he tugged his scarf up over his nose, squinting through the soft snow still falling. Hunting in this was going to be a bitch.

It was slow going at first, his worry over Alex slowing him down and dividing his focus, but after awhile, the powder under his feet and falling all around him became his world and Oren felt his stress slipping away, one step at a time.

He hiked up the side of the hill and halfway along the ridge before stopping for a breather. If it hadn't been snowing, he'd probably have been able to see the grey plume of his chimney smoke from where he was, but instead his world was soft white and dark trees on either side, the only color his brown snowsuit.

Oren glanced back once more toward Alex and his house, then plunged down off the ridge and into the trees. He moved more on instinct and memory than sight or sound, guided by the shape of the branches and his internal compass, floating through the trees with almost no noise.

He'd missed this, he had to admit. The freedom of moving, being dependent on no one but himself, the clean air and the stark white and raven black around him.

He reached his deer stand, unbuckled his snowshoes, and swung himself up into it, then settled in to wait, binoculars at the ready.

The problem with hunting, he admitted to himself after the first hour, was that it gave him too much time to think.

Specifically, time to think about Alex, with his porcelain bones and eyes that had seen too much, the way his hair fell over his brow as he looked up from under his lashes, hope and curiosity on his delicate features. Oren wanted to touch that hair, run his fingers through it, see if it was as soft as it looked. He *wanted* Alex, he knew, and touching him would be the worst thing he could do.

You're an asshole for wanting it, he told himself silently, and shifted his weight. *Think about something else.*

"Buy me dinner first." The boy's voice was light, amused, and Oren jerked his eyes up.

"What?

The boy raised a mocking golden eyebrow. "If you're going to undress me, you have to buy me dinner first."

*Oren could feel himself firing scarlet. "I'm—
I wasn't—"*

*"I'm Ben." The boy held out a hand and
Oren fumbled and dropped his math book. It hit
with a loud thud that echoed in the auditorium,
and Oren wanted to sink into the floor. Ben's
other eyebrow went up.*

*Oren finally managed to find the coordina-
tion to take his hand. It was big and warm,
slightly sweaty, and the skin was soft, his fingers
strong as he clasped Oren's hand and shook it.*

*Ben's mouth quirked, and Oren knew he was
in trouble.*

OREN CLOSED his eyes for a minute. *God,
Ben, I miss you. You would love Alex.*

A BRANCH SNAPPED, and Oren's attention
returned to the clearing in front of him. A
small buck, half-obscured by the falling snow,
had stepped out of the other side and was
considering whether to cross the open space.
Oren shifted his weight soundlessly and
brought the rifle to bear, resting it on the
frame of the deer stand and sighting down the
scope.

The deer was motionless for a long time,
nearly head-on to Oren. A bad angle, easily
missed, and too far away for Oren to risk

firing and wounding him. It had to be a clean shot.

He waited, stiff muscles and numb fingers forgotten, as the deer made up its mind and stepped delicately into the clearing. One step. A second. Then a third, and it was broadside to him. Oren let out the breath he'd been holding in one slow exhale and at the end, he pulled the trigger.

The rifle report was deafening, frightening birds from the trees in a thunderous uproar, snow showering after them. Oren barely noticed. The deer jumped straight up in the air, landed, stumbled. Took two steps and went to its knees. Oren slung his rifle on his back, grabbed his pack, and jumped out of the stand as the deer toppled onto its side, pulling his hunting knife from his pack and approaching, cautious of the still twitching hooves.

※

IT TOOK him a lot longer to get home hauling a three hundred pound deer. Eventually, he fashioned a rough sled and slung the carcass on it, dragging it behind him as he trudged over the snow. He was aching and exhausted by the time he reached the door, every muscle complaining, but he kicked off his snowshoes with quick movements, leaving the deer where it was momentarily. He needed to tell Alex he was home first.

But when he stepped inside, the house was

dark and cold. Dread stretched uneasy elbows in his chest.

"Alex?" There was no answer. "Oh no," Oren whispered. "Alex? Alex!" *If he left again…* There was no way to track him with the snow coming down even heavier now, and Alex wouldn't last ten minutes, even with his crutch. Oren stripped his gloves and ran upstairs. The bathroom and bedroom were both empty.

"Goddammit." Oren turned to hurry back out, intent on searching downstairs, but a movement from the wardrobe caught his eye. The doors were slowly opening. Oren bolted toward it, his heavy boots loud and jarring on the wood floor, to see Alex's blond hair as he cautiously emerged. Oren went to his knees next to the wardrobe, relief turning his joints to water. "It's me," he said, holding out a hand. "It's me, I'm back."

Alex scrambled out and into Oren's arms, nearly knocking him backward with the force of his embrace. He clung to Oren's neck, trembling, but didn't say a word.

"Were you…" Oren closed his eyes, afraid he knew the answer. "Were you in there the whole time?"

Alex nodded against Oren's shoulder.

"Oh, honey," Oren whispered, and tightened his grip. "I'm so sorry. But look, I'm home, I'm here. Everything's okay."

Alex eased back a fraction to look into Oren's eyes. He was only an inch away, and it would have been so easy to bend down and seal their mouths together—Oren cleared his throat and attempted a smile.

"I bagged a deer," he said, and Alex looked briefly confused.

"Bagged—oh, shot?"

Oren huffed a laugh and let go so he could get up and pull Alex to his feet. "Yeah. I've got to get him into the garage and on the rack. Do you want to watch?"

Alex nodded, but Oren had the distinct feeling it was more to do with not wanting to be separated from Oren than actually watching what he was doing.

The deer carcass had a blanket of fresh snow on it, still growing, and Oren picked up the sled handles and towed it into the garage as Alex held the door for him. Inside it was cold but not quite freezing. Oren lowered the winch and strapped the deer's hind legs into it. He raised it until the buck's front legs were an inch off the floor, then set a big bucket under its nose.

"I have to drain it," he told Alex, still standing by the door. Oren pulled his hunting knife out and cut the deer's throat in one clean slice. Thick, dark blood flowed sluggishly down its chin and into the bucket in a crimson curtain.

Alex made a strangled noise and fumbled for the door handle. He was outside before Oren could react. *Shit.* Oren dropped the knife and went after him. He found Alex on hands and knees just outside, retching in the snow.

"Fucking hell, Alex—" Oren went to his knees beside him again. "I'm sorry, I didn't think, are you okay?" He held out a hand, unsure Alex would want to be touched.

Alex hunched his shoulders, trembling. "Sorry, Oren. Sorry—"

"Don't apologize," Oren said. He took a chance and rubbed Alex's back. "You must have seen so much during…. I'm sorry."

Alex turned and leaned into him and Oren wrapped his arm around Alex's waist.

"Let's get out of this cold," he said gently. "I'll butcher the deer on my own later, once it's drained." He helped Alex up and into the house, up the stairs to the bathroom. "You'll want to brush your teeth," he said, pointing at the mirrored cupboard. "I keep a couple of extra toothbrushes so I don't have to go to town often. Help yourself to one and I'll get you dry pants."

He came back with another pair of pants and Alex's crutch. Alex's face was white as he leaned against the sink, looking at himself in the mirror. Oren knocked on the door with one knuckle.

Alex turned. "Do you need… help? With deer?"

Oren shook his head. "I've done it myself plenty of times. If you *want* to help, you can, but—"

Alex was shaking his head too. "I am sorry, but I think—"

"Here." Oren held out the crutch and pants. "Come downstairs when you're ready.

Let me just make sure the deer is draining properly and I'll be back."

WHEN HE GOT BACK INSIDE, Alex was on the couch, eyes on the door. Oren smiled at him.

HE WOKE the next morning to Alex bending over him.

"The snow has stopped," Alex said, excitement vibrating through his voice. "Oren, it has stopped!"

Oren sat up, rubbing his eyes, and forced a smile through the dread that sank in his stomach like a stone. "That's great. As soon as it starts to melt, we can go."

"Tomorrow?" Alex was very nearly thrumming with tension, his entire body tense and focused.

Oren hesitated. "Maybe. It depends on how warm it gets today."

Alex sagged and Oren touched his shoulder.

"Hey," he said gently. "I promised, okay? As soon as possible."

"Okay," Alex said. He smiled suddenly, his brown eyes lighting up. "Your hair is… ridiculous."

Oren felt at it, realizing it was standing on end and trying in vain to smooth it down.

"Not everyone is as gorgeous as you when they roll out of bed in the morning, pal," he said.

To his amazement, Alex blushed at that, ducking his head as dimples appeared. "*Esti frumos tot timpul*," he said.

"What now?" Oren asked.

"Nothing," Alex said, standing. "Will you show me… how to make your pancakes?"

"Yeah, I can do that," Oren said, narrowing his eyes, but Alex kept his own gaze averted as Oren stood up.

ALEX PROVED to be a terrible cook, beating the batter for too long and unable to determine when the pancakes were ready to be flipped, but Oren gamely ate the finished products, swallowing the bits of charcoal and giving a thumb's up when Alex looked at him anxiously for approval.

"So what do you do today?" Alex asked, resting his elbows on the table and cradling his chin on his hands.

"Gotta get back to work on those orders," Oren said. "Now that the snowstorm's over, I'll be expected in town soon anyway, so I need to have the first few ready to go."

"Can I—"

"You want to come with me again?" Oren asked, a little startled. "Sure, kiddo, but aren't you getting bored of my workshop by now?"

"It has you in it," Alex said simply, and

Oren caught his breath as the butterfly under his ribs stirred.

"Sweet-talker," he said, keeping his tone light, and stood to clear the dishes. "Can you read English?" he asked over his shoulder. "It occurs to me that if so, I have bookshelf upon bookshelf that you can choose from."

"Da," Alex said, stacking the dishes still on the table. "I am not—fast, but I can read more than I speak. At home, in village, I always had book in my hands. Mihai teased, said the world would go past me and I would never know."

Oren laughed as he washed the dishes and cleaned the counters. "That sounds about right."

ALEX PICKED out one of Oren's favorites, a sci-fi action story based loosely on the battle of Rorke's Drift, and Oren looked at him in surprise.

"Are you sure?" he said. "Not that I'm casting aspersions on your intelligence, but the vocabulary might be a little over your head."

Alex shrugged, tucking the crutch under one arm and the book under the other. "If I do not understand, you can explain to me, yes?"

"Sure," Oren said. *As if I could say no to that face.*

AT SOME POINT, he reflected halfway through the day, carefully setting a tiny windowsill in place, Alex might stop surprising him, but it didn't seem like it would be any time soon.

Alex was curled up in his chair, the blankets pulled up almost to his chin and the book in front of his nose as he devoured it.

He'd asked for clarification of a few things at the very beginning of the story, getting a feel for the setting, but from there he'd barely looked up, turning page after page in rapt absorption.

Over dinner, Oren shook his head, smiling to himself. "Liking it?"

"So much," Alex said without looking up. "Although I do not understand some things. Why do the Krai eat anything?"

Oren laughed quietly. "Haven't you ever met someone who'll inhale anything set in front of them?"

"Yes," Alex said, finally glancing away from the book. "Mihai is like that. He will eat anything."

"Well, the Krai just take it to an extreme. Plus it's funny, and the author uses that to excellent advantage."

Alex hummed thoughtfully. "And the… how do you say it—di'Tay…"

"The di'Taykan?"

"Da," Alex said, cutting his green beans into several pieces and impaling them on his fork. "I do not understand why they have so much sex."

Oren couldn't help his snort at that. "It's a biological imperative."

"A what?"

"Uh… means that they literally need sex to live."

Alex grimaced and put his fork down. "I would not… want to be like that."

Oren watched his face, the play of shadows under Alex's haunted eyes. "Has it ever been good for you, Alex?" The words were out before he could think better of asking the question.

Alex looked up. "It has been… not bad sometimes." He lifted one bony shoulder, toying with his fork. "I could pretend I was—away. Not in my body, you know?"

Oren swallowed grief and nodded. "You wanna go read by the fireplace?"

"If you will be there," Alex said.

"Let me just wash up and we'll do that," Oren said.

He looked out the window as he set the pot to soak. The snow was definitely melting, which meant that by tomorrow the roads might be navigable. Alex was going to insist on leaving in the morning.

Dread swelled in Oren's chest, making it hard for him to breathe. Who knew what Alex was walking into, going back for Mihai like this?

He dried his hands off and climbed up to the living room to where Alex was already on the couch, his good leg tucked underneath him and book propped on his knee.

Oren chose a book off the shelf at random, barely seeing the titles, and sat down beside him. Alex immediately shifted his weight, curling up against Oren's side like a cat, solid and warm under Oren's arm.

I can't, Oren thought helplessly. *I barely know him and I already can't bear to think of losing him.*

"Bi—bio—biological… what is other word?" Alex asked.

"Imperative," Oren managed. "Biological imperative."

"Da," Alex murmured, rubbing his cheek on Oren's shirt. "This is my… biological imperative." He sounded half-asleep already, drowsy and content.

Oren closed his eyes. He had absolutely no idea what to do.

When the fire had burned to its embers, Oren finally stirred and reluctantly dislodged Alex, by now fully asleep, in order to carry him to bed. Alex turned his face into Oren's chest, his arms around Oren's neck, and Oren climbed the stairs and set him gently in the bed, pulling the covers up into place.

Alex snuggled down into the pillows with a sigh and Oren couldn't resist smoothing his hair off his forehead.

"Donkey," he whispered.

HE MADE himself as comfortable as possible on the couch, questioning yet again why he'd bought it in the first place as he tossed and turned, a spring poking him in the ribs and another in the thigh.

AROUND THREE AM, Oren heard a tinkle of glass downstairs and he sat up straight, wondering if he'd dreamt it. It came again and he swore to himself and nearly fell off the couch in his haste to get upstairs. He wasn't exactly a high risk for break-ins, this far out. It had to be Andrei, back now that the roads were clear.

Alex was sound asleep, his mouth lax and soft, hand tucked beneath his cheek.

Oren took a deep breath, forcing himself to calm so that he could think.

Andrei's men didn't know the layout of his house. They'd likely search the downstairs first. But that wouldn't take long and then they'd be upstairs and the game would be up. Oren had minutes, at best.

Thank *God* he was a neat housekeeper. There was literally no sign of Alex's presence in the house except for Alex himself, which meant that all Oren had to do was figure out what to do with *him*.

He scooped Alex up out of the bed and ran for the wardrobe as Alex startled awake in his arms.

"Oren, what is it, what is wrong?"

Oren was too busy dragging the heavy doors of the wardrobe open to answer immediately. He set Alex on the lip of the beast and then felt for the spring.

"C'mon, c'mon," he said through his teeth. It gave under his searching fingers and the false bottom of the wardrobe slid back silently.

Alex stared at him, his eyes huge in the moonlight.

"There are men in the house," Oren said. "I need you to hide in here. Can you do that?"

Alex swallowed hard and nodded jerkily. He crawled into the space, drawing his legs to his chest and wrapping his arms around them, pressing his face against his knees.

Oren reached in and touched his hair and Alex looked up at him. "It's going to be okay," Oren said. "I won't let them touch you. Don't make a sound, no matter what you hear."

He slid the bottom back into place over Alex's form without waiting for a response and swung the doors shut, turning to survey the room. He could hear feet climbing the stairs, and he grabbed the baseball bat that he kept by the bed and charged into battle.

He burst from the bedroom with a blood-curdling scream, swinging the bat wildly, and heard a meaty thud as the bat connected with someone's shoulder and they grunted in shock and pain.

Oren swung again, but the bat stopped mid-arc and then it was ripped from his hands and fingers were crushing his windpipe as he was forced back into his bedroom.

Oren clawed at the hand on his throat,

choking and gasping, blackness crowding his vision.

"Let him go, Mikhail," someone said, sounding bored. "Boss said not to kill him."

The force on his throat abruptly eased and Oren went to his knees, tears streaming from his eyes as he dragged in air.

Someone was bending over him, flattened nose and small eyes, thin, cruel mouth—the goon who'd been with Andrei.

"Remember me?" he said.

Oren managed a nod.

Mikhail was busy tearing Oren's bedroom apart, behind him. Something shattered and Oren flinched.

"Where is he?" the goon asked.

"Who?" Oren rasped.

"Bedroom empty, Nikolai," Mikhail called.

"Check the bathroom and kitchen," Nikolai said. "I'm going to talk to our friend here." He hauled Oren to his feet by his shirt with frightening ease and tossed him onto the bed.

Oren sprawled across the mattress as Nikolai loomed over him.

"Where is he?" he repeated.

"I don't know who you're talking about," Oren managed through the fear threatening to choke him.

"Where is it?"

Oren blinked at that, thrown. "Where's… what?"

"You know what," Nikolai said. "Tell me

where it and the *syavka* are, no one has to get hurt."

"I—I have no idea what you're talking about," Oren said, struggling to get his elbows beneath him.

Nikolai gazed at him contemplatively. "Boss thinks you're lying. Me? I think I don't care. I get paid either way. But it doesn't look good, I think. So you tell me what you know, yes?"

"I don't know *anything!*" Oren said, dragging himself upright. He prayed that Alex would have the sense to stay silent and not give himself away. There was no point in both of them having to suffer.

"Maybe not," Nikolai agreed. "So let's find out." He punched him and Oren's world went dark.

OREN WOKE up flat on his back with Alex on the floor beside him, patting his face and sounding like he was trying to stifle tears.

"Please wake up," he was saying, over and over. "Please, Oren."

Oren groaned. It felt like he'd been run over by a semi with a grudge. The entire left side of his face hurt, and from the state of his ribs, Nikolai had left a parting gift or two there as well.

Alex caught his breath. "Oren?"

Oren opened his eyes. Alex was leaning over him, his cheeks wet.

"Ow," Oren said.

"Don't move," Alex said, his tone anxious.

"Man, that guy's got a punch like a mule," Oren said, feeling his face gingerly. "Are you sure they're gone?"

Alex nodded. "You should lie down right... in right way."

"As long as you stay with me," Oren said, his eyes still closed.

"I will," Alex said, his voice wobbly.

He did his best to help Oren to his feet and onto the bed, both of them swaying dangerously, and Oren made himself comfortable with a groan, sinking into the pillow.

"I'm so sorry," Alex whispered miserably.

Oren opened his eyes to see Alex looking at him from a few inches away, brown eyes full of guilt.

"I should have come out," Alex managed. Even in the dark, Oren could see the tears in his eyes. "I should have stopped him."

"How?" Oren countered. "You're a buck twenty soaking wet and a stiff breeze would knock you over. Besides, you're what he wanted. If you'd come out, he'd have killed me and taken you. I'd rather be bruised than dead." He reached down, groping for Alex's hand and twining their fingers together. "Andrei's a piece of shit," he said. "You're not to blame for his actions. He'd have done this whether you were here or not."

"Oren," Alex whispered.

"Rest," Oren said. "We'll talk more in the morning."

7

———

ALEX WAS AWAKE BEFORE OREN, making his way to the bathroom silently. Oren woke as Alex returned and sat up in the bed, yawning and stretching.

"Ow," he said again, feeling delicately at his face.

"How do you feel?" Alex asked anxiously, sitting down on the bed beside him.

"Sore," Oren said, dropping his hand and smiling at him. Alex didn't return the smile. "How about some breakfast?" Oren said, and Alex shrugged.

Oren stayed close on the way to the living room, but Alex was getting fairly adept with the crutch and made it to the couch on his own without a problem, collapsing in his usual boneless sprawl on one end.

Oren sat down next to him. Breakfast could wait—whatever was bothering Alex needed to be addressed first.

"Spit it out," he said.

Alex looked confused. "Spit—what?"

"What's going through your head?" Oren said. "Something's obviously eating you up inside. Tell me what it is."

Alex drooped, his entire body a curve of guilt. "Is my fault," he whispered. "All of this, because of me."

Oren reached out and took his hand, rubbing his knuckles gently with a thumb. "That's not true," he said. "You want to blame someone, blame Andrei."

Alex shook his head, staring at the floor as a tear slid down his cheek. "Mihai was sold because of me," he managed, the words sounding as if they were being dragged from his throat.

Oren went very still. "What does that mean, Alex?"

Alex finally looked up, more tears spilling down his face. "I fail—my high school exams. Math—I cannot get it, I just—" He swiped at his cheeks with the back of his free hand. "Teacher say I can retake tests, get diploma in three months, but without it, I cannot get job, I cannot help our parents."

Oren was beginning to put the pieces together. "So you failed to get your high school diploma, which meant you couldn't get a decent job, which meant you couldn't help with the family's income."

"Yes," Alex whispered. He sounded like he'd swallowed shards of glass, his voice broken and hoarse. "My parents could not…

feed us. They would have sold me, I think, but they knew I would fight. And anyway, I was too old. Mihai… Mihai was so young, so gentle and—" He broke off with a sob and Oren pulled him into his arms, down onto the couch next to him.

"Let it out," he said against Alex's ear, clasping him tight. "Let it all go, sweetheart, you'll feel better for it. You've been holding it in for too long."

Alex made an awful choked wail and began to weep in earnest, his frame heaving in deep sobs as he grieved.

Oren could feel hot tears on his own face as he held him, wishing he could do something to ease Alex's pain, to fix the situation.

Alex burrowed closer, clutching at Oren's shirt as his weeping began to taper off into gentler tears. Oren rubbed his back, crooning nonsense into his hair until Alex finally lifted his head.

"I am sorry," he whispered.

Oren couldn't resist dropping a kiss on his nose, making Alex's eyes go almost comically wide.

"Don't be silly," he said. "Besides, I'm a lot cheaper than a therapist."

Alex's brows drew together. "You are so… *strange.*"

Oren laughed a little, wincing as it pulled on his abused facial muscles, and sat up. "So I've been thinking."

Alex sat up too, watching Oren's face, his expression wary.

"I think we should go to the police today," Oren said.

"*No*," Alex said instantly, recoiling so fast he nearly fell off the couch.

Oren went after him, capturing both his hands. "Alex, *listen* to me."

Alex was shaking his head desperately, terror on his face. "They will kill him, Oren, when they see police, they will—"

"We'll make sure they understand not to go barging in guns blazing," Oren said. "We'll tell them the situation, *make* them see how much danger Mihai and the others are in, and that they have to handle it properly." He gestured to his face. "I think between the two of us, we have more than enough evidence that these are bad guys and they'll need to take it seriously."

"But—"

Oren tightened his grip. "Sweetheart, look at me."

Alex looked up at him, his eyes still wet.

Oren smiled, a touch rueful. "I'm no one's idea of a hero, honey. Do you really think that you with your broken ankle and me with my skill at making pancakes would be able to storm the castle on our own?"

"It is house," Alex said.

Oren couldn't help his laugh as the butterfly in his chest stirred again. "God, you're adorable. I just meant that the two of us on our own aren't exactly a force to be reckoned with. The cops can help, Alex, that's what they're there for."

Alex looked at him, eyes dark and unreadable. "You do not want to be found either."

Oren let go of Alex's hands and sat back on his heels, running his fingers through his hair. "I guess everyone has to stop running sometime."

"No." Alex shook his head. "That would be... my fault too. No."

"Grown man," Oren reminded him. "My decision."

"But Oren—"

"Sweetheart," Oren said, cupping his face. "Stop talking. My mind's made up."

Alex brought a hand up, holding Oren's hand in place against his cheek, and went to his knees. He moved slowly, giving Oren plenty of time to stop him as he lowered his face until their lips were touching. Oren's breath hitched and he forgot how to breathe, caught up in the warm slide of Alex's lips and tongue, fingers threading through his hair, one thumb stroking his cheekbone. Alex kissed hesitantly, as if afraid to make a mistake, but he tasted like sunlight and absolution and Oren could have stayed there forever, sitting awkwardly on the side of the lumpy couch as he memorized Alex's mouth.

Finally, though, Alex broke away, his breathing ragged, hand still cradling the back of Oren's neck, and Oren pressed their foreheads together.

"Okay," he finally said. "So that happened."

"I'm sorry," Alex whispered.

"For a kiss that incredible? Why?"

Alex sat back, mouth unhappy. "You said —and then I kissed you even though you don't want—"

Oren took his hand. "Sex and kissing don't have to go together. I've been wanting to kiss you for a long time. And I mean… I *do* want sex, sometimes, but… you're not ready."

Alex tilted his head. "You do not want sex —but you want kiss—to kiss me?"

"If that's okay with you," Oren said, smiling at him.

"Da," Alex whispered. "You are… good kisser."

"Only when I have a good partner," Oren murmured, turning his head to kiss him again and something that had been niggling at him since Nikolai's visit slotted into place as neatly as a puzzle piece.

He jerked away, making Alex flinch. "The dishes!"

"What?"

"The dishes," Oren repeated. He lunged, scooping Alex off the couch in one smooth motion and turning to run for the stairs as Alex clung to his neck. "There aren't any signs of you in the house, except the kitchen," he panted as he pounded up the steps. "Two plates, two bowls… two—cups…"

Alex's eyes went wide. "You think—"

"Yeah," Oren gasped. He nearly dropped Alex on the bed in his haste, tripping over an apology, but Alex waved it off.

"Get what you need," he said, his eyes

huge with fear. He wrapped his arms around himself. "Where… will we go?"

"Into Cheyenne," Oren said as he flung the wardrobe open and grabbed a heavy backpack from it. He stuffed a sweater and Alex's pills into it, cramming the first aid kit on top and slinging it over his shoulder. "We have to go *right now*. They could be back at any minute, there's no telling when they'll realize what they saw."

"What if they don't?"

Oren stopped for a second. "Do you really want to take that chance?"

Alex hesitated and then shook his head.

"Me either. Let's go."

He bundled Alex into his arms again, hating the way he was trembling.

"It's going to be okay," he said as they put coats on and he carried him down the stairs to the garage. "I won't let them touch you."

Alex said nothing, holding onto Oren's sweater with an almost desperate tightness.

But when they got to the garage, it was to the sight of the jeep with all four tires slashed, sitting on its rims.

Alex made a quiet noise and put his head on Oren's chest as Oren stared blankly at his vehicle.

"Plan B," he said finally. "We hike to town. Maybe hitchhike, if we can find someone dumb enough to be out in this besides murderous Russians."

"You cannot carry me all the way to

town," Alex protested. "It is too much, Oren, you must not!"

Oren grinned at him, baring his teeth. "Fucking watch me."

He dropped the pack on the floor and set Alex on the hood of the jeep. "Piggy-back," he said, turning around.

"Piggy-*what?*" Alex said, sounding on the verge of a breakdown.

"Sorry," Oren said. "Get on my back, sweetheart, just slide right on, there you go, like that." He guided Alex into position, keeping him in place, and then bent and picked up the pack. "Can you put this on your back?"

Alex wriggled awkwardly into the backpack, struggling to keep his balance as Oren held still. When he was ready, Oren strode out of the garage, the cold hitting him like a slap in the face and making him gasp. He felt Alex huddle against his back, tightening his grip.

But as he turned to make his way down the driveway toward the road, the unmistakable rumble of an engine floated up through the trees below them and they both froze.

"It's them, it's him," Alex said urgently against his ear.

"Probably," Oren said. He began backing up the slope toward the tree line, watching the road. Their only chance was if he could hide them in the trees, get them out of sight and make a run for it. Even weighed down by an extra hundred and fifty pounds, Oren liked their odds. He'd seen the dress shoes the

Russians had been wearing, and he hadn't spent two years lumberjacking in the north for nothing.

Alex was clinging to him so tightly Oren's oxygen was threatened. He patted Alex's thigh as he climbed. His thighs were burning, his lungs aching, but everything in him howled *hurry, hurry, they're coming back.*

"Need to be able to breathe, babe," he said, keeping his voice light.

Alex loosened his grasp instantly, babbling an apology.

"You watch the house until we're out of sight, tell me if you see them," Oren told him, and began to climb in earnest.

The tree line wasn't far—he'd built his house in the middle of the forest very deliberately, after all. But every nerve twitched as he covered the open ground, knowing they were exposed to anything and everything like this.

"I see—" Alex said just as a gun barked and a half-second later, a bullet zinged past their heads.

"*Fuck.*"

Oren started running in a zigzag pattern, bobbing and weaving as someone fired again and then a third time. Both bullets whined harmlessly off into the forest, a man shouted, and then they were under the trees and Oren was taking them deeper in, ducking branches and skirting trunks as the world grew dark around them, the sun blotted out by the branches above them.

Alex held on, his head down and legs

wrapped around Oren's waist, sticking like a burr.

Oren kept going, the burn in his thighs settling into a steady ache. He hadn't pushed himself this hard in years, but it wasn't something the body easily forgot. He found himself falling back into the regular breathing, in-out-in with his footsteps, moving like a shadow through the trees without making a sound.

He climbed for several hours before he stopped, even though there hadn't been any sounds of pursuit.

Finally, though, he found a small clearing that fit his purposes and he knelt, easing Alex to the ground.

When Oren turned to face him, Alex was unsuccessfully trying to wipe tears away.

"Is it your ankle?" Oren asked. "You should take a pill—I don't know how much longer I'm going to hike, but it'll be awhile, and you're going to be wiped."

Alex shook his head, gulping air, and pointed at the valley. Puzzled, Oren looked where he was pointing.

A huge, black plume of smoke was billowing lazily up from below them. There was only one structure large enough to create a pillar of smoke that big, Oren realized, his stomach turning over. *His house.*

"Oh no," he whispered. His house, *his* house, the one he'd built himself from scratch, fueled by determination and dollar store noodles and endless sleepless nights, was going up in flames right now, with all his beloved creations inside it. Turned to ash, destroyed in an instant.

Alex buried his face in his hands. "I am so sorry, Oren," he sobbed.

"We need to keep going," Oren heard himself say, as if from a great distance.

Alex dropped his hands and drew a deep breath, squaring his shoulders and nodding. He got to his knees and Oren helped him climb back into position.

Oren stood and began walking again without looking behind him.

HE CLIMBED for several more hours, numb with grief, but by the end of it, he was beginning to put things in perspective. He'd built it once. He could build it again. He was still healthy, still young and strong and talented, not to mention good at what he did and in high demand. He didn't *have* to survive on dollar store noodles this time when he was rebuilding—he could make it better than it had been before. That one basement door that had always hung a little crooked could be fixed. The plate glass windows he'd wanted but hadn't been able to afford last time were within his reach this time. And his fireplace— he almost smiled to himself. His fireplace with its one crooked stone would still be there.

Alex was silent, still holding on but saying nothing, and finally Oren decided they'd gone far enough.

He chose another small clearing and stopped, kneeling and letting Alex slide to the ground.

"How are you feeling?" he asked.

Alex lifted a shoulder. "It matters not." His voice was small, defeated, and Oren realized he'd spent the last several hours blaming himself for everything that had happened.

He took Alex's hands in his, startling Alex into looking up. Oren was smiling when he did.

"How are you feeling?" he repeated.

"I—" Alex closed his mouth and hunched his shoulders.

"You're in pain," Oren guessed.

Alex hesitated and then nodded jerkily, and Oren let go of him to pull the backpack off his shoulders and rummage in it for the bottle. He handed Alex a pill and waited for him to swallow it before beginning to unpack the rest of the bag.

"I don't have a tent, unfortunately, and my go bag is geared for one," he said as he set out items. "So we'll have to share the sleeping bag, and I'll either have to fish or scavenge food for us, because the MREs I brought won't feed both of us for long. Luckily, I do have a fishing line and hooks in here."

Alex watched him, clearly puzzled. "What is... go bag?" he asked.

Oren hesitated in shaking out the waterproof sleeping bag. "I guess it was bound to come out sooner or later. Let's have dinner and I'll tell you, okay? I don't think it's safe to have a fire yet, they could be out looking for us."

They sat down cross-legged on the sleeping bag and Alex chose the chicken alfredo MRE. Oren opted for the lasagna, and they both began to eat.

"I'm twenty-six years old," Oren said between bites of lasagna. "And when I was seventeen, I killed a man."

8

———————

HE WAS aware of Alex's eyes on him, but he kept his own gaze fixed firmly on his meal as he spoke.

"His name was Ben. We were... best friends." *Golden, laughing Ben, star of track and field, charming and funny and guaranteed to have anyone smiling within minutes of meeting them. So different from Oren, with his strange sense of humor and gangly limbs, ears that stuck out and hair that wouldn't lie flat.*

"I don't know what he saw in me. Maybe it was just that I was a good foil for him." Oren shrugged, stabbing a bite of pasta.

Alex tilted his head. "Foil?"

"Uh... I made him look better. He was tall and handsome and smart, I was short and awkward and weird. Puberty wasn't very kind to me, and I wasn't exactly popular in school. I have no idea why he decided to be friends with me."

Alex took Oren's hand, his fingers warm and solid. "He was… good person?"

Oren nodded, his throat closing up. "The best person," he managed.

"That is why," Alex said simply.

It was a minute before Oren could speak again. Finally he drew a breath.

"The night before we graduated high school, we went to a party. Everyone was there, it was nuts. There was a lot of drinking, of course, but I was driving, so I didn't have any, I stuck to the juice. Only I didn't realize it wasn't just juice—someone had spiked it."

Alex opened his mouth but Oren beat him to the punch.

"Spiked—they'd put alcohol in it. I didn't taste it, it was really sweet, and I didn't realize."

"Oh," Alex said softly, putting his food on the ground and wrapping his arms around his midriff.

"Yeah," Oren said. "I knew something was wrong, but Ben was even worse off than I was. He was in no condition to take the wheel. I was taking him home, and he lived way out in the country, about fifteen miles outside town. I used to complain about how far out he lived, and he'd spend the night at my house more often than not." *Sleeping on my bed, his hair tickling my nose, his arm draped across my waist in a careless sprawl—*

Alex shifted a little closer. His eyes were luminous in the moonlight, his skin almost translucent except where the bruises still mottled the surface, an ugly reminder of what they were running from.

"What happened?" he asked.

"I wrecked the truck," Oren said bluntly. "I was wearing my seatbelt. Ben wasn't. I don't know how fast I was going, but I wrapped the truck around a tree. Killed him on impact. Broke my leg in three places, my wrist, collarbone, a few ribs." He closed his eyes.

"How long were you… with him? Until found?" Alex asked.

"It was around three AM when it happened," Oren said. "My phone was smashed, and I couldn't get to Ben's. It was probably busted too, considering what had been done to him. We were found by someone going to work, around eight."

Alex shivered, sliding another inch nearer. "All that time, alone with…." He hunched his shoulders. "I am sorry, Oren."

"Are you cold?" Oren said abruptly.

"A little," Alex said. "It matters not."

"No, come here." Oren pulled Alex into his arms, opening his jacket, enveloping Alex's slender frame in its downy warmth. Alex shuddered and relaxed against him with a shaky sigh.

"Oh. Thank you."

Oren pressed his cheek to Alex's silky hair. "Anyway, Ben's parents pretty much owned the town. They had businesses all over, Ben's dad was running for office, they were heavy hitters, and they'd never liked Ben being friends with me."

"They blamed you." Alex's voice was soft, beginning to slur with exhaustion and the drugs kicking in.

"Yeah, they did. Convinced the DA—sorry, district attorney—to throw the book at me. Try me as an adult, get every single charge levied against me they could think of. My parents weren't rich, they couldn't afford a decent lawyer, so I took a plea deal."

"What is plea deal?"

"I basically pled guilty to all the charges and they gave me a reduced sentence—twenty years. Because I was a juvenile, and I didn't cause problems, I was given parole in a little over a year. I was home before I was nineteen."

Alex had relaxed against him, his limbs sleep-heavy and loose, his breathing slow and steady, and Oren held him and gazed up at the stars, cold and frozen above them.

"I miss you, Ben," he whispered. "I couldn't stand it. It was like being flayed alive, every time I went outside, every look I got, every whisper, every turned shoulder and hissed comment. I wanted to die too. I wanted to be with you, I didn't want to be alone anymore. You'd left me, just like you'd promised you'd never do."

So he'd left too. Kissed his mother's cheek as she dozed in front of her crossword puzzle, the television flickering silently over the room, and shouldered his bag.

He'd caught a ride out of Texas on the first semi that was willing to take him, uncaring where it was going, just needing to *go*, to get away.

Alex stirred, rubbing his nose against Oren's arm. "Mihai," he whispered, and squirmed into a more comfortable position.

Oren held him a while longer, but finally his back began to protest, and he sighed, maneuvering Alex upright.

Alex blinked at him, his eyes drowsy, and Oren fought the urge to kiss him yet again.

"Sorry," he murmured. "But we need to actually get in the sleeping bag or we'll freeze to death before the night's half over."

"Alright," Alex agreed, dreamy and placid, and allowed Oren to help him into position inside the bag.

"Lucky for you I got the roomy bag," Oren said, sliding in next to him and zipping it up. It was snug, but they both fit.

Alex made a drowsy noise and turned toward him, pressing his face into Oren's collarbone. His breath tickled Oren's skin and Oren was pretty sure he was already asleep again.

Oh help, Oren thought yet again, and fell asleep himself.

Oren woke up alone in the sleeping bag. He jolted upright, adrenaline flooding his system in a sickening rush as he looked wildly around the clearing, but there was no sign of Alex.

Oren scrambled out of the bag, swearing under his breath. Alex didn't even have his crutch—how far could he have gotten?

The ground crunched beneath his feet and Oren's breath hung in front of him in tiny, frozen clouds as he cast around for footprints. He found Alex's trail easily enough, striking out to the south and east, back toward Cheyenne.

"You brave, stupid—" Oren set his jaw and plunged down the hill, slipping and sliding on the icy patches, his arms flailing wildly as he struggled to keep his balance.

Alex had gotten farther than Oren had expected, simply by peeling a piece of bark from one of the trees outside their camp and using it as a sled. Unfortunately for him, it had overturned into a snow bank and he was struggling to drag himself out and get back on it when Oren caught up to him.

Oren lost his balance and nearly fell head-first into the snow next to him, managing to stop himself by hooking an arm around the trunk of the nearest tree. His fall aborted, he dragged himself back to his feet and spun on Alex.

But his anger evaporated when he realized that Alex was on his knees, both arms over his head, braced for a blow.

"Oh no," Oren said, going to his knees himself. "Alex, *no*. Look at me, sweetheart, can you do that?"

Alex lowered his arms slowly, tears streaking his cheeks. He was trembling, and Oren had a feeling it was only partly to do with the way his clothes were thoroughly soaked.

"Oren," he whispered. "He will kill you. I *had* to go."

"You left for me, didn't you?" Oren said gently.

Alex nodded, wiping his face with the back of his hand. "Andrei is… evil, Oren. He will—I had to."

Oren reached for him, unable to bear it any longer, and pulled him into his arms. Alex fell against him with a stifled sob, his delicate frame shaking, and Oren held him, rubbing his back and crooning an old lullaby his mother had sung to him.

It took several minutes and a few repetitions of the song before Alex was quiet, but finally Oren eased him away and looked at him. Alex's eyes were red, his nose running, and he ducked his head, shame on his face.

Oren cupped his chin, tilting Alex's head back up. "I'm in this for good now," he said. "Andrei burned my house down, Alex, you really think he'd let me just walk away?"

Alex lifted a shoulder. "If I gave myself back, give him the—"

"No," Oren interrupted. "No, that's not how guys like him operate. He won't let me live. I've seen too much, and that means I need to be silenced. Besides." He smiled, a little rueful. "I've never been one to back down from a bully. Drove Ben *crazy*, the way I was always throwing myself in the middle of fights and breaking up dogpiles."

Alex's brow creased and Oren couldn't

help his laugh, but he cut off abruptly as a thought occurred to him.

"Give him the what?"

Alex hunched his shoulders, turning his head away.

Oren caught his chin, gently pulling his face back around. "Give him the what, Alex?"

"I—" Alex swallowed hard. "I took something. When I run."

Oren's stomach sank as Nikolai's questions began to make sense. *Where is it?*

"What did you take?"

"Thumb drive," Alex whispered, holding his fingers up about an inch apart. "Had all Andrei's… clients."

"You took his little black book," Oren said, swallowing nausea.

Alex nodded miserably.

"Oh boy," Oren said. He bent over, bracing his hands on his knees, and concentrated on breathing deeply. "Okay. *Oh* boy. Oh holy shit, oh my god."

"I'm sorry," Alex whispered.

Oren lifted his head. "No, I understand, really. You needed insurance."

"Insurance, da," Alex said. "That he would let us go."

"So where is it?" Oren asked. "If it had been on you, I'd have found it. Unless you—" He broke off, peering closer at Alex, who snorted an unwilling laugh.

"Is not inside me," he said. "Is in Cheyenne. Safe. I will get it… and Mihai.

Same time. I will give him back this, and he will give me Mihai. That is plan."

"Fair enough," Oren said, standing up. "Right now we have to get back to camp and pack our stuff so we can get going. We've lost a fair amount of daylight."

He helped Alex onto his back and started up the hill. The uphill trek was a lot more difficult than the downhill one had been, and he had to stop several times to rest, not running on adrenaline like he'd been yesterday.

"I'm sorry," Alex said after the second time Oren stopped to catch his breath.

Oren patted his thigh. "When we get to camp, I'm going to make you a travois. It'll be easier on both of us. I should have done it last night, but I fell asleep and forgot."

He reached camp without further rests and eased Alex down onto the sleeping bag. "Have axe and rope, will travel," he said cheerfully, digging in his pack for both items. He spent some time selecting the right size tree limbs and then arranged them in an X pattern, lashing them in place and adding two more limbs in a rung formation lower down.

"It's not going to be the most comfortable," he said as he worked, "but I think I can rig the sleeping bag between the poles to act as a sort of seat to hold you while I walk."

Alex watched, fascinated, moving obligingly when Oren needed the sleeping bag to put in place.

"We're going to get you another crutch,

too," Oren told him. "I'm sorry I left yours behind."

"You were in hurry," Alex said, smiling. "Where are we going?"

"Well, we can't go to Cheyenne, obviously," Oren said as he tested the travois' strength. "So we're going to Laramie."

"You cannot walk all the way to Laramie, Oren!" Alex said.

Oren grinned at him. "I've walked farther. It's only… what, fifty miles from Cheyenne proper? And I was already two miles outside the city limits, plus I covered easily five miles last night, so I got a nice jump on it already. We're close to 211 by now. We'll hit that and then it'll be smooth sailing. Maybe we'll be able to hitchhike into town."

"You are crazy," Alex said.

"Entirely possible," Oren agreed. "Hop on, let's give this puppy a go."

Alex gave the travois a suspicious look, but he maneuvered himself to his knees and sank onto the seat, tucking his feet up underneath his body. Oren took a lap around the clearing, watching over his shoulder, as Alex gripped the edges of the travois with both hands, but Oren's work held firm and he set it down triumphantly after one circuit.

"I'm a genius," he said complacently. "I'm gonna pack the escape bag and then we'll get going."

Alex reached out a hand, catching Oren's wrist and pulling. Oren went to his knees next to him and silence fell between them. Alex's eyes were huge and dark, the tip of his nose pink from the cold, and he lifted his hand and cupped the back of Oren's neck, bringing their mouths together sweet and slow.

Alex's lips were cold, a startling contrast to the warmth of his tongue, and he threaded his hands into Oren's hair, catching and tugging gently as he took his time exploring Oren's mouth.

Oren's knees were getting damp in the snow and the angle was awkward, but he thought distantly that he could have stayed there forever, lost in Alex's spell, lips and tongues sliding against each other, Alex's breath feathering warm across his cheek in soft, hesitant puffs.

Finally, though, Alex broke away, one hand still wrapped around the nape of Oren's neck, his breathing ragged.

It took Oren a minute to find his voice. "What—ah… was that for?" he finally managed.

Alex's mouth curved up and he lifted a shoulder. "For luck?" he suggested.

Oren blinked, thrown, and then started to laugh. The stress of the past several days caught up with him in a rush and he collapsed in a helpless heap, half in Alex's lap, as he howled with laughter. "Did you just—you did, you just Star Wars'd me!" he gasped.

Alex stared down at him as if he'd grown a second head. "You are doing it on purpose now," he said, his tone accusing.

Oren wiped away tears and pushed

himself upright, putting a hand on either side of Alex's face and kissing him again, quick and soft.

"I'm not," he managed, swallowing another rush of giggles. "I swear I'm not. I'll explain if we make it out of this alive, okay?"

Alex leaned up into another kiss. "Okay," he said. "We should go."

"Yeah, definitely," Oren said. "Just one more thing," and kissed him again.

He couldn't stop smiling as he walked, pulling the travois over the rocky ground, casting quick glances over his shoulder to make sure Alex was in place.

It took several hours of hiking through the trees before he finally hit 211, the broad, flat farm road that ran between Cheyenne and Laramie in a meandering, lazy sprawl through the hills.

Oren set the travois down and bent over by the side of the road, his hands on his knees as he labored to catch his breath.

"How you doing, Alex?" he asked between gulps of air.

The answer was slow in coming. "I am alright." His voice was faint, and Oren straightened to take a look at him.

Alex was white as a sheet, the circles under his eyes so dark they looked like bruises, and he swayed as he gripped the edges of the travois with both hands.

Oren swore and felt his forehead. "You're trying to get sick on me again, aren't you?"

"I am not trying to," Alex protested softly, squeezing his eyes shut.

"Figure of speech," Oren said. "Okay, listen. I'm going to walk along the road, see if anyone's out and about. If they are, I'm going to try and get us a ride into Laramie. Listen to me—Alex, pay attention, can you look at me?"

Alex looked up at him, beads of sweat on his forehead.

Oren fought down a surge of worry. "You're a hiker I found in the woods, okay? You fell and that's where you got those bruises. You're on vacation, you're a tourist, you don't speak much English."

A glimmer of amusement sparked in Alex's eyes at that. "I... *don't* speak much... English."

Oren cupped his face briefly. "Keep that sense of humor, sweetheart. Now hold on, I'm going to start walking again."

He was able to set a much faster pace on the flat tarmac, although he had to be careful not to slip on the icy patches. Alex curled up in a ball on the sleeping bag seat and Oren put his head down and pushed himself as hard as he could, setting a speed he knew from experience he could hold for hours without collapsing.

The sun was well overhead when he stopped for a break around midday, but Alex barely roused when Oren set the travois down.

Oren decided that since there'd been no signs of pursuit, it was safe to risk a small fire, and he started a pot of snow boiling to sterilize it.

He managed to get Alex to swallow a little of the cooled water, but then his head drooped and he was out again.

Oren gulped down a cold MRE and shouldered the pack, getting back on the road as quickly as possible.

He was relieved to see a road sign helpfully telling him that Laramie was only twenty-seven miles away, and he put his head down and walked faster as Alex lay in a motionless ball.

Close to sunset, Oren knew he was pushing himself near the brink of exhaustion, but he hadn't seen a single car on the road. He wasn't sure Alex would survive another night in the cold, not in the condition he was in.

"Oren," Alex said, his voice weak.

Oren set the poles down and hurried around them to kneel on the pavement next to Alex. "Yeah, Alex, I'm here."

Alex reached a wavering hand out and Oren took it, worry surging through him at the heat radiating off Alex's skin.

"Promise me," Alex managed.

"If you're going to make me give you a deathbed promise, you can save it," Oren said, his throat tight. "You're not dying, you hear me?"

Alex ignored this. "Save... Mihai," he whispered, his eyes beseeching.

"We're going to do that together, sweetheart," Oren said, and then headlights bathed them in brightness and Oren caught his breath and stood up, waving his arms frantically, and the car was pulling over and doors were opening, people spilling out and voices raising in concern.

THE RIDE into Laramie was a blur. Their saviors were an older couple named George and Rosie. George drove like a bat out of hell, all his attention on the road, his broad shoulders hunched in fierce concentration while Rosie, tiny and birdlike, twisted in her seat to talk to Oren and Alex.

Oren was crammed up along the door, Alex half in his lap, still mostly out of it, his eyes closed and his face turned in against Oren's abdomen.

"What *happened?*" Rosie asked, all warm, fluttering concern.

Oren struggled to marshal his thoughts, unable to think of anything but how frail and helpless Alex looked. "I—I was hiking, and I found him in the woods. He doesn't speak much English, but he said he was out hiking too and he fell. He broke his ankle, and I think he has pneumonia or something. Please, sir, can you go any faster?"

"I go any faster, they'll be picking us up off the road in pieces," George said gruffly, but a minute later, the city limit sign flashed by.

"We'll be to the hospital in a jiffy," Rosie

said comfortingly, but Oren barely heard her, bending over Alex again.

"Hold on," he breathed against his burning-hot cheek. "Hold on for me."

AT THE HOSPITAL, things devolved into a lot of shouting and bustling as Alex was yanked forcibly from Oren's arms and bundled onto a gurney, disappearing behind a bevy of blue-scrubbed nurses through double swinging doors.

Oren staggered, bereft, and Rosie caught his arm and guided him to a chair.

"Here you go, son, now you sit yourself down here and rest, you're worn through clear to the bone, look at you!"

"Stop fussing, Rosie," George rumbled from somewhere above them.

Rosie made a rude noise. "Someone's got to, George, this poor boy obviously hasn't had anyone take care of him in ages!"

Oren couldn't help his weak laugh. "I just need to catch my breath," he said. "I'm okay, really. Thank you both, so much."

"Well, I'm just glad we could help," Rosie said as a nurse approached, clutching a clipboard.

"We need you to fill out some paperwork on the young man who was just admitted," she told Oren, who blinked at the clipboard.

"He… doesn't have insurance," he said.

"None at all? Are you sure?"

"Positive. We talked… a bit. He doesn't have a job or income, I'm sorry. His name is Alex, but…." Oren trailed off. "I don't know his last name, actually."

"Alright," the nurse said. "Sit tight, we'll be back with you soon."

'Soon' turned into hours. Oren fell asleep in the corner, his head at an uncomfortable angle, arms crossed as he waited for any news.

Finally, another nurse gently woke him. "Are you the one who brought the hiker in, sir?"

"Yes," Oren said before he was fully awake, jerking upright. "Yes, that's me, do you have news? How is he? Is he okay?"

The nurse, a Hispanic woman in her fifties, smiled at him. "He had a broken ankle and quite a few other injuries—do you know anything about this young man?"

Oren swallowed a rush of fear. "I… not really. Why?"

"The injuries present as signs of severe systematic abuse, done to him over a period of years. He's also been raped quite recently as well. Did he say anything to you, maybe indicate who might have done this to him?"

Oren shook his head, nausea welling up. He'd known, of course, known what Alex had gone through, but hearing it put so bluntly made him want to throw up all over again.

"Well, he's not a minor, and he refuses to say who did it to him, so there's really not much we can do. He mostly keeps asking for you. Will you come talk to him?"

Oren shot to his feet. "Why didn't you lead with that?"

The nurse looked taken aback, but she stood and ushered him through the halls, her crepe-soled shoes squeaking on the floors, to a small room.

Oren stepped inside and the nurse shut the door behind him after making a gentle motion toward the bed. Oren took a step forward; swallowing hard at the sight of Alex in the bed hooked up to various machines, looking terribly young and vulnerable, his eyes closed.

Oren sank down onto the chair beside the bed as Alex's forehead creased and he turned his head on the pillow, his eyes still closed.

"Oren," he whispered.

"I'm here," Oren managed around the lump in his throat. "You gonna open your eyes, you donkey?"

Alex's mouth curved up and he opened his eyes. "*Bună*, Oren."

"I'm going to assume you just said hello and you didn't profess your undying love for me or something," Oren said, somehow keeping his tone light. He took Alex's hand, careful not to tangle any of the wires and cords that trailed off his bed, and brought it to his lips. "How are you feeling, gorgeous?"

Alex twisted his hand to cup Oren's face, stroking his cheekbone with his thumb. "Am... better. Sleepy."

"You go ahead and rest, okay? I'll be as close as they let me be."

Alex's hand tightened on Oren's at that. "Don't leave… me, Oren."

"I won't," Oren said. "The nurse might kick me out for a few minutes here and there but I'll be back the second they let me through the door. I won't leave this hospital until you're with me, okay?"

"Do you promise?" Alex whispered, his eyes drooping shut.

"I promise," Oren said gently. "Go back to sleep, sweetheart."

Alex's grip slackened, lashes fanning dark across his pale skin, and Oren sat quietly, holding his hand and watching him sleep as he worked on a plan for the next few weeks.

9

____

THE NURSE'S name was Maria, and apparently she had a soft spot for waifs, because when she came in a few minutes later and found Oren holding Alex's hand, her eyes softened and she turned on her heel and left.

She was back in another few minutes with a steaming cup of coffee and handed it to Oren, who cradled it gratefully in both hands and inhaled the fragrant steam as Maria checked Alex's vitals.

"Can I stay with him?" Oren asked quietly.

Maria glanced at him over her shoulder as she straightened Alex's IV lines. "It's against hospital policy," she said briefly.

"Please," Oren said, swallowing hard. "I'm —he doesn't have anyone else. He barely speaks English. I feel... responsible for him."

Maria smoothed Alex's blankets over his legs and sighed. "The dayshift starts at six AM sharp. As long as you're not in the room when the shift changes, I'll clear it with the day nurses." She fixed him with a sharp look. "You stay out of the way, keep him quiet, and don't make any noise yourself, do you understand?"

Oren nodded, gratitude thick under his tongue. He couldn't get the words out, couldn't explain why it was so important, but Maria seemed to understand. She patted his shoulder and pointed at the empty bed on the other side of the room.

"Get some rest," she said. "You look nineteen different flavors of exhausted yourself."

Oren drained the coffee as Maria finished tidying Alex's bed and left the room, letting the door swish shut behind her. He stood and kicked his shoes off, suddenly unable to think of anything but the clean, cool sheets of the empty bed, and stumbled across the room to crawl under the covers.

Sleep claimed him almost immediately, the steady beeping of Alex's machines pulling him under.

HE DREAMED OF A WEEPING CHILD. Oren thought vaguely that they were in a bus terminal or somewhere similar—it was packed with people, faceless throngs that jostled and bumped him as they pushed by.

The crying was ahead of him, he thought, so he struggled in that direction, using his elbows to force his way through the crowds, his breathing growing labored as he fought for each inch forward.

The people vanished, growing suddenly insubstantial and misty as smoke, wisping away into nothing, and Oren stumbled and fell forward, landing on his knees in a meadow.

A little boy was crouched in front of him, both hands over his face as he wept.

"Hey," Oren said, holding out a hand. "Hey, it's okay, why are you crying?"

Alex twisted, tears streaking the dirt on his face, his brown eyes huge and full of grief. "I've lost him," he whispered.

"Who?" Oren asked, but he knew the answer.

Alex covered his face again, looking impossibly small and defenseless, and his shoulders shook.

OREN CAME BACK to awareness slowly, consciousness seeping in around the edges. The machines were beeping, someone was talking on the phone at the nurses' station outside, and… Oren sat up straight in bed as he realized that Alex was crying, curled up in a ball on the mattress, his thin frame heaving with the force of his sobs.

Oren nearly fell off his own bed, scrambling across the room to touch Alex's shoulder. "Alex, wake up," he whispered.

Alex flinched away and lifted his head,

awareness filling his eyes. "Oren—"

"Scoot over," Oren said.

Alex obeyed mutely and Oren slid onto the mattress, gathering Alex into his arms and pulling him close, careful not to dislodge his leads. He could feel Alex trembling against him, taking deep gulps of air in an attempt to keep from breaking down again, and Oren rubbed his arm.

"Let it go," he said quietly. "Let me take it from you for a little while."

Alex pressed his face into Oren's chest and let the tears flow as Oren held him, crooning lullabies quietly to him in snatches of half-remembered Spanish until Alex's sobs tapered off and he was finally still, limp and exhausted, in Oren's arms.

When Maria came in an hour later, Alex was asleep again, still cradled in Oren's embrace. She stopped and arched a brow.

"Not what I had in mind," she said, her tone low.

Oren grimaced apologetically. "You said keep him quiet. This was the only thing I could think of to do."

Maria woke Alex up gently and took his vitals, clicking her tongue at the fever he was still running. Then she left again, cocking a warning brow at Oren again on her way out the door.

Alone, Alex burrowed sleepily against Oren's chest. "*Dragă*," he murmured.

Oren rubbed his arm, feeling the fragile

bones beneath Alex's too-warm skin. "Hey you. How are you feeling?"

"Better," Alex said through a yawn. He rubbed his nose on Oren's shirt, making Oren smile. "I am sorry I wake you."

Oren scoffed quietly. "As if I'd pass up a chance to get my arms around you."

Alex hid his face in Oren's chest and huffed a soft laugh.

"Was it a nightmare?" Oren asked after a minute.

Alex nodded without lifting his head. "It is no matter," he mumbled. "You can go back to you—your bed."

"Nah, I like this one," Oren said. "I think I'll stay here."

This time Alex did lift his head, looking up at him suspiciously. His face was pale, washed out by his illness and the moonlight that bathed them both through the window, and his curls tumbled forward over his eyes. Oren had to fight the by-now very familiar urge to kiss him yet again.

Instead he just smiled. "Would I be right in assuming that you and Mihai always shared a bed while in Andrei's employ?"

Alex blinked, clearly parsing out Oren's English in his head.

"Sorry," Oren said hastily. "I meant, did you and Mihai sleep in the same bed?"

"Oh." Alex nodded. "Da. Always together."

"That's what I figured," Oren said. He was

in the perfect position to press a kiss to Alex's forehead, so he did, letting his lips linger on the soft skin near Alex's temple as Alex turned into it, clutching Oren's shirt, his eyes sliding closed.

Oren let the silence spin out, cradling Alex against him. *You're safe*, he told him wordlessly, over and over. *You're not alone.*

Finally, Alex relaxed into sleep, Oren's shirt still between his fingers, and Oren held on.

He woke a few minutes before six and slid out of the bed without waking Alex. He could hear the nurses talking at their station, and he used the bathroom quickly and then slipped out the door, heading for the cafeteria.

His wallet had been in his pocket when they ran, and nearly a decade of hiding from the authorities had taught Oren caution, if nothing else. He had cash on him, which he used to pay for breakfast.

Settling in at a table in the corner with his oatmeal and fresh fruit, Oren glanced at a newspaper someone had left behind as he began to eat.

His attention sharpened immediately when he read the headline.

ONE PRESUMED DEAD IN FATAL HOUSE FIRE

Oren nearly knocked over his orange juice grabbing for the paper and scanned it as he held his breath.

Oren Asher, a talented local artist, is believed to have perished yesterday in the blaze that consumed the house he built himself, sources tell this paper. Mr. Asher was a respected member of the community, his creations in high demand, and there is no word yet from authorities on whether or not the fire was accidental or intentional.

There was more, but Oren put the paper down, staring unseeingly at the people getting breakfast, his mind spinning.

He didn't linger over his meal, knowing Alex would get upset if he woke up and Oren wasn't there. He grabbed a blueberry muffin off the buffet bar for Alex, figuring it would be a nice addition to whatever they gave him for breakfast, and headed back up.

Sure enough, he wasn't even back to the room when he heard the commotion, Alex's voice raised in terror cutting clearly through the hubbub.

Oren dropped the muffin and broke into a run, slamming the door open and falling through to behold two nurses holding Alex down as he thrashed.

"Where's that *fucking* sedative?" one of the nurses shouted.

Oren hurled himself at the bed and Alex sobbed as he saw him, struggling to reach for him as the nearest nurse caught Oren's arm and stopped him.

"Oren, *please*—" Alex was weeping outright and guilt shivered through Oren's chest.

"You don't need a sedative," Oren said, jerking away. "Let me go, let *him* go, he's okay, I promise, just let me hold him!"

The nurse let go and Oren scrambled for the bed, gathering Alex against him.

"Hey," he whispered, "I'm sorry, sweetheart, I had to be gone for shift change and I just went to get some breakfast. I'm here, I'm right here."

Alex clutched at him, trembling. "I woke up, you were—I thought—"

"I'm so sorry, baby," Oren said, rubbing his back. "Everything's okay, I promise. I'm here. You're not alone."

He was dimly aware of the nurses talking in low tones at the foot of the bed, but they didn't say anything to him, so Oren kept his attention focused on Alex, whose trembling was beginning to lessen, although he was still clinging to Oren desperately.

"Well, I brought you a muffin," Oren said, making his tone light, "but I dropped it when I heard the ruckus."

Alex burrowed a little closer somehow. "What is… ruckus?"

"Noise, commotion," Oren said against his hair. "I thought I was back in the circus there for a minute."

Alex lifted his head, his brows drawing together. "You are… teasing me."

Oren dropped a kiss on his nose. "Can't get anything past you, I see!"

Alex blinked, startled, and his eyes narrowed. Just as Oren realized the nurses had left and they were alone, Alex leaned in and pressed their lips together.

Oren could taste the salt from Alex's tears on his mouth, and that alone was enough to make him hesitate, but Alex made a noise in the back of his throat, soft and supplicating, and Oren closed his eyes and kissed him back.

It was slow and sweet and gentle, like the summer wind on his face or that warm satisfaction in his chest when he got a carving just right.

Alex broke it first, kissing along the line of Oren's jaw. "*Dragă*," he whispered between kisses, his lips soft on Oren's stubble, dragging along his skin and making Oren shiver.

"What does that mean?" he asked.

Alex tilted his head back and considered Oren's face, a tiny smile curving his lips. "Maybe someday I tell you," he said, and tucked his head back against Oren's shoulder.

Oren cupped his skull, feeling the hard curve of bone, smiling against his hair. "So I was getting breakfast and I saw something interesting in the paper. They covered my house burning down, and I'm assumed to have died in the fire."

Alex stiffened and Oren pushed him away just far enough to see his face. Sure enough, there was guilt written all over it.

"No, none of that," Oren said firmly,

pulling him close again. "My house is *not* your fault, do you hear me?"

"Happened because of me," Alex whispered, his voice muffled against Oren's shirt. "Is my fault."

Oren tightened his grip. "Even if that were true, it wouldn't change how I feel."

Someone knocked on the door and Oren lifted his head, startled. One of the nurses from earlier was standing there and she motioned toward the hallway.

"Hey, I have to go talk to a nurse," Oren said.

Alex looked at him, clearly worried, and Oren cupped his cheek briefly.

"I'll leave the door open and stay where you can see me, okay?"

Alex hesitated, chewing on his lip, but finally nodded, and Oren slid off the bed to join the nurse in the doorway.

She was short, plump, and graying, with fine lines bracketing her eyes and a name tag that said ROSA.

"What the hell was that?" she said, her voice quiet but her eyes fierce.

Oren winced, glancing at Alex, who was watching them anxiously. "He's got… separation issues. He was treated really badly before we met, it's left him with some severe emotional… baggage. I think he's sort of… latched onto me as his security blanket?"

"Looks like you've done some latching of your own," Rosa said dryly.

Oren just shrugged, sending Alex a smile

that said *everything's fine.* "Look, I'm sorry about that. Maria told me not to be here during shift change and I thought it'd be okay if I nipped down and got some breakfast. I didn't realize he'd freak out quite so… thoroughly."

Rosa made a *harrumph* noise and crossed her arms. "What exactly is your relationship to that young man?"

"We're friends," Oren said. "We were in the woods together for several days and we formed a… bond."

Rosa lifted an eyebrow. "And you've known him for how long, exactly?"

"I'm not sure how that's any of your business," Oren said. Alex was watching him, clearly still worried, and Oren sent him a reassuring smile. "Look, is there a problem?"

Rosa shrugged. "We don't have any insurance on file, and he has no way of paying his bill here. The law states we have to treat him anyway, but the hospital isn't going to spend any more on him than it absolutely has to. Which means that he's going to be discharged probably today or tomorrow at the latest. I just want to make sure he has somewhere to go and that he'll be taken care of."

"He will," Oren said. "He's got me, I'll take care of him, I promise."

"And your name is?"

On the verge of telling her, Oren remembered that he was supposed to be dead. "Osmundo Acevedo," he said. "Can I go? He's starting to get upset."

"Don't go far," Rosa said, but Oren was already back inside the room, letting the door close behind him.

He'd been telling the truth—Alex had been looking more and more upset throughout the conversation, and he visibly relaxed as soon as Oren closed the door and crossed to the bed.

"Sorry about that," Oren said, sitting down in the chair next to him and taking Alex's hand. "Would you like me to go back to the cafeteria and get you a muffin? They have some blueberry ones that are pretty good, and the bran looked tasty too."

"*No,*" Alex said, gripping Oren's hand tightly and shaking his head. "Please, don't leave."

"Okay, sweetheart, I'll stay," Oren said. A thought occurred to him. "Alex… what's your last name?"

"Costea," Alex said. "Why?"

"I just… realized I didn't know it," Oren said. He cleared his throat. "So the paper reported that I died in the fire, right?"

Alex nodded.

"That's a really good thing," Oren said. "It means that whoever shot at us, it definitely wasn't Andrei."

Alex's brows knitted. "What do you mean?"

"I mean, if it had been Andrei, he'd have chased us down and made sure we were dead," Oren said. "The fact that we're still alive means that he sent his goon—what was his name?"

"Nikolai," Alex whispered.

Oren squeezed his hand. "And Nikolai decided we'd freeze to death and there was no point in chasing us. He must have told his boss we were dead."

Alex's eyes opened wide. "*Oh.*"

"Yeah," Oren said, grinning at him. "If Andrei thinks we're dead, we've got the drop on him. Or at the very least, a slight advantage. But there are a few things we're going to have to do before we storm the castle."

"It is *house*," Alex protested.

Oren put his head down on the bed and gave in to the laughter. It felt good to let it roll through him in delighted waves, and when he looked up to see Alex scowling at him, arms crossed across his chest, it just made him laugh harder.

"I'm sorry," he finally managed. "I promise, when this is all over, we're going to rent The Princess Bride and you're going to actually start understanding at least half my references. In the meantime, there's something else I wanted to ask you."

He wiped the tears of laughter from his eyes and took Alex's hand in both of his. "Alex Costea, will you marry me?"

10

ALEX'S MOUTH fell open and he jerked his hand out of Oren's, sitting up straight in the bed. "*What?*"

Oren rubbed the back of his neck. "Not quite the reaction I was hoping for," he admitted ruefully.

"You can't—you do not know—Oren, *why?*"

Oren held out his hand, asking silently for Alex to take it, and after a long moment, Alex did. Oren squeezed it gently.

"Couple of reasons," he said. "The main one being, once this is all over, if we're married, you can't be deported as easily. It's still a possibility, especially if we get someone looking to make an example of us, but it could help. And since Mihai is your brother, and he's still a juvenile, then hopefully the judge will see that you're the best person to take care of him, considering your parents *sold* him and all."

"So he would not be deported either?" Alex asked, that crease back between his eyebrows, and Oren wanted to kiss it, smooth it away, but he just nodded.

"That's the theory, anyway. We might get a hardass judge, but it's still going to help. Plus, this way once everything has blown over, *if* our gamble works and the judge is lenient, and *if* you're willing to stay married to me for a few years, then you can apply for citizenship of your own and stay in the country. If you want, I mean."

Silence fell except for the beeping of the machines as Alex considered and Oren waited, holding his breath.

"Why?" Alex asked again finally, and Oren knew what he meant. *Why do this for me?*

Oren sighed. "I was a loner in school, before I met Ben. He… pushed me out of my shell, forced me to have fun in spite of myself. He was good for me, and when I lost him…." He swallowed around the grief and Alex's hand tightened on his. Oren lifted a shoulder, trying for a smile. "I ran away from life," he managed. "I hid from the world, until you fell into my lap."

Alex said nothing, watching him with an intensity that bordered on unnerving.

"Ben would want me to do this," Oren whispered. He could feel tears prickling at his eyelids, but he blinked them back fiercely, focusing on Alex's face. "And I want to help you, Alex. You've saved me as much as the other way around."

Alex covered his eyes with his free hand, drawing his knees up to his chest, and Oren tightened his grip.

"Alex, sweetheart, say something."

Alex's shoulders shook. "I do not deserve—"

"Bullshit, yes you *do*," Oren interrupted. "You deserve the world, *catâr*."

"Is… legal?" Alex asked, lowering his hands. "What if—"

"I have an idea about that too," Oren said. "It is, strictly speaking, not exactly *legal* in the broadest sense of the word—" He cut off at the confusion on Alex's face. "It's not legal, no. But I think I can still make it work."

Alex took a deep breath. "*Bine*," he said abruptly. "I will marry you, Oren."

"Yeah?" Oren breathed, feeling a smile spreading across his face. "You will?"

Alex nodded, matching his smile as he ducked his head. "Da, Oren."

"Oh, thank God," Oren said, half-laughing as he stood up. "Can I kiss you?"

"Always," Alex said, reaching for him. "You never have to ask, Oren."

Oren slid onto the bed and gathered Alex against him, feeling his frame go instantly boneless, loose and trusting in Oren's arms.

Alex tilted his chin up, eyes heavy-lidded and mouth parted in anticipation and Oren caught his breath.

"God, you're so beautiful," he whispered, and kissed him.

Alex's lips were pliant and warm and sweet under his, his hand on Oren's face, soft against the several days' growth of stubble there.

Oren broke away first, laughing deep in his chest. "I need a shave something awful," he said. "I must look like such a hobo."

Alex smiled at him, amusement and affection lighting his brown eyes. "I do not know what hobo is, but *esti frumos tot timpul.*"

Oren pointed a finger at him. "You said that before, after the bedhead incident. What does it *mean?*"

Alex laughed outright, ducking his head to hide his face against Oren's chest. "It means… you are beautiful always."

Oren's breath caught in his chest. "Keep that up and I'm going to have to kiss you again, you sweet-talker."

"Do you promise?" Alex asked, a smile curving his mouth.

"Well, you don't have to talk in Romanian to get me to kiss you, but I love hearing you speak your language, yeah," Oren said.

"In that case," Alex said. "*Îmi place cum râzi când spui glume proaste.*"

Oren kissed him again, smiling against his lips. "What does that mean?"

"Roughly… I love your laugh when you tell a bad joke."

Oren laughed, pulling him closer. "I've got more," he said. "Just you wait, you'll see. What else?"

"*Îmi place cum mă ții*," Alex murmured. "I love the way you hold me."

Oren closed his eyes. "Oh help," he said out loud. "I'm not going to survive you, am I?"

"*Te iubesc*," Alex whispered.

When he didn't translate it, Oren pushed him gently away. "Gonna tell me what that one means?"

Alex shook his head, smiling. "Maybe someday. Kiss me, please?"

"Gladly," Oren said, and bent to obey.

It was a while before they spoke again, content to hold each other and take respite in the dim peace of the room, but after about twenty minutes, the door swung open and an unfamiliar nurse walked in with a basin under one arm. She was young, close to Alex's age, slim and blonde, a smile on her face.

"Room service!" she said cheerfully. "Time for a bath, Mr. Costea. I'm Bethany, your day nurse."

Oren and Alex sat up and Oren nudged Alex with an elbow. "Sponge bath from a pretty nurse, it's your lucky day!"

Alex gave him an unimpressed look and Oren grinned, glancing up to see a matching expression on Bethany's face.

"Make yourself scarce," she suggested.

Oren glanced back at Alex, who looked alarmed.

"Don't leave," he begged.

"I need a shower," Oren told him, taking his hand. "I'll use the bathroom here, you'll be able to hear me the whole time, okay?" He looked back at Bethany. "You wouldn't happen to have a pair of scrubs I can borrow, would you? My wardrobe is sadly lacking at the moment."

"I'm sure I can come up with something," Bethany said, hooking a thumb toward the bathroom.

Oren took the hint and scrambled off the bed, giving Alex an encouraging smile as he went.

He was delighted to find a new disposable razor tucked in with the soap and shampoo and he shaved in the shower, letting the hot water pound his muscles and soothe out the knots.

When he was done, he opened the door a crack, wrapped in a towel, to discover a set of scrubs on the floor waiting for him, and he snatched them up and closed the door again to pull them on.

His mouth fell open when he shook them out and discovered they were pale pink and printed with tiny fish all over the fabric. Bethany's idea of revenge for the sponge bath crack, Oren supposed, grinning.

Freshly dressed and clean-shaven, he stepped out of the bathroom to see Alex sitting up in bed watching for him as Bethany took his vitals.

"Looking sharp," Bethany observed, her lips twitching.

Oren flexed. "Takes a man truly secure in his masculinity to pull off an ensemble like this. What do you think, kiddo, do I make it work?"

Alex looked him up and down, fighting a smile of his own. "Very... sexy."

"I'm irresistible," Oren said to Bethany, who snorted and began gathering up the bath supplies.

"If you say so, pal. Mr. Costea, try and get some rest. You'll probably be discharged tomorrow if you can keep that fever down."

"I will try," Alex told her seriously.

Bethany smiled at him, her expression softening. "You do that."

She left the room and Alex held out his hand to Oren, who took it and slid onto the bed with him, gathering him in.

"How are you feeling?" he asked against Alex's hair.

Alex lifted a shoulder. "Clean."

"Clean is good," Oren agreed. "Never underestimate the power of being clean."

Alex sighed. "So strange."

Oren just laughed and kissed his hair. "Learn to deal with it. Do you think you can nap? You need to rest and heal before they kick us out of here."

Alex nodded. "If you will... stay?"

"Of course," Oren said gently. At some point they were going to have to address Alex's abandonment issues, he knew that, but now was not the time.

He stayed in the bed until Alex had relaxed into sleep and then carefully disentangled himself and padded back to the clothes he'd left on the bathroom floor, digging in the pockets to retrieve his carving knife and the half-finished whittling.

Then he settled himself in the chair by the window where he had the best light and could see Alex's face when he woke up, and began carving again.

He lost himself in the meditative feel of the silky wood under his fingers as he teased out the image in his head and watched it take shape in his hands, glancing up to check on Alex every once in awhile as he worked.

Bethany came in at lunchtime carrying a tray, which she set on Alex's roll out table. Her eyebrows shot up when she saw what Oren was doing.

"You can't have a *knife* in here!" she hissed.

Oren blew a wood shaving off the pine as Alex stretched and yawned, his eyes finding Oren first.

"The blade is barely three inches long," Oren said, holding it up so Bethany could see it. "You'd have to be seriously intent on doing harm to inflict any sort of damage with this baby."

Alex drew his knees up as Bethany scowled at Oren and Oren sighed and sheathed the knife, shoving it in his pocket.

"There. Happy? The weapon of mass destruction is put away."

Bethany switched her focus to Alex, who flinched. Bethany grimaced and relaxed her posture, putting on a smile. "I brought you some lunch, Mr. Costea. Do you feel like eating?"

Alex glanced at Oren, who smiled at him but said nothing, and finally nodded, allowing Bethany to raise the bed so he was sitting up.

"While you eat, I need to speak to your friend in the hall," Bethany said.

Alex tensed, his fingers going white on the fork, and Oren stood up, touching his knee under the blanket.

"I'll stay where you can see me," he told him, and followed Bethany out.

She crossed her arms over her chest, giving him a formidable glare. "I don't like you," she informed him.

Oren winced. "I'm sorry about the sponge bath comment, if it helps. I was just trying to make Alex smile and I didn't mean any disrespect."

Bethany relaxed a little. "Fine," she said. "Rosa told me what happened earlier, so I'm not going to make you leave him. She also told me that you're responsible for his care once he's discharged."

Oren nodded. "Yeah, I'm… I'll take care of him."

"Alright. He's been given a broad spectrum antibiotic, tested for any STDs he might have considering his sexual history, and he's clean.

He has to keep that fever down, though, or he's not going anywhere."

"I understand," Oren said.

"He needs serious mental therapy, do you understand *that*?" Bethany asked. "The second you can, get him to a therapist, preferably one who speaks his language. He's got more baggage than my mother in law on vacation."

"I know," Oren said, rubbing his neck. "Believe me, I know. And I'll find him someone, I promise."

Bethany inspected his face. "I think you will," she said finally. "Your story's got holes I could drive a truck through, and there are a dozen things about Mr. Costea that cause alarm bells to go off in everyone's heads, but you really care about him, don't you?"

"Yeah," Oren said, smiling at Alex, who was watching them from the bed. "Yeah, I really do. Was there anything else?"

"That's it for now," Bethany said. "Get back in there and remember what I told you."

Oren saluted, making her snort, and ducked back into the room.

"Is everything okay?" Alex asked.

"Everything's fine," Oren said, sitting down by the bed. "She just wanted to make sure I knew what kind of treatment you'd been given. What's lunch?"

Alex poked at it dubiously with his fork. "Am not... sure."

"Hospitals," Oren said, grinning at him. "If the doctors don't kill you, the food will."

"Still better than Romania," Alex said.

"Mihai was going to come to States after school, to study at college here."

"By himself or were you going to go with him?"

"He wanted me to come," Alex said, drawing his knees up to his chest. "I was going to play piano and be famous, he said."

"That can still happen, if you want it to," Oren told him.

"I do not care about famous," Alex said, resting his cheek on his knee. "I just want to play piano and be with Mihai… and you."

Oren took his hand where it lay on the bed and Alex curled his fingers around Oren's palm. "That can definitely happen," Oren whispered, and Alex smiled at him.

THE REST of the day passed peacefully, with Oren taking every spare moment to work on the carving when he knew Bethany wouldn't catch him. Alex slept, and watched him, lying on his side, his eyes calm and the shadows lying a little lighter on his face.

"I'm sorry I didn't bring your book," Oren said at one point.

Alex smiled, clearly half-asleep, his hand tucked under his cheek. "Is alright. Perhaps you can tell me how it ends?"

"Don't you want to read it yourself?"

"Da," Alex said through a yawn. "But I like to listen to you talk."

"And you call *me* crazy," Oren said, smiling at him. "Where did you stop?"

"The ship had crashed in swamp," Alex said, wriggling to get comfortable. "Haysole… was hurt. I like Haysole."

"He's one of my favorite characters," Oren agreed.

"He reminds me of you," Alex murmured, his eyes drooping.

"Stunningly attractive and effortlessly funny?" Oren said. "Yeah, I get that a lot."

Alex huffed a quiet laugh. "Bad jokes to hide real feelings," he said, and closed his eyes.

Oren winced. He hadn't been expecting quite that level of sharp sightedness. He cleared his throat. "So the ship crashes in the swamp and Torin has to get her people to safety, including the wounded—"

He talked until he was sure Alex was fully asleep and then put the wood carving back in his pocket along with the knife and crawled into the bed opposite. He had some rest to catch up on himself.

ALEX WEEPING WOKE him up and Oren sat straight up in the bed, looking for the danger. Realizing there was none, he slipped off his mattress and hurried to Alex's side.

"Mihai," Alex sobbed. He was curled in a ball, knees drawn to his chest, still deeply asleep and trapped in the dream that held him. "Mihai, *no*—"

Oren touched his shoulder. "Alex, wake up."

Alex flinched violently away, catching himself on the bed railing as Oren backed up to give him space.

"Just me," he said, keeping his voice low and calming. "Just plain old Oren, I promise, you're safe."

"Oren—" Alex's voice cracked and he sounded like a child, lost and terrified.

"Can I hold you?" Oren managed.

Alex nodded, jamming a hand against his mouth to stop another sob as Oren slid onto the bed and gathered him up.

"I cannot stop dream—dreaming," Alex whispered. "I dream Mihai—I see him dead, over and over, Oren, every time I close eyes he is there."

Oren cradled him, tucking Alex's face against his shoulder and holding him close. He could feel the tremors wracking Alex's lean frame, the way he was keeping himself together by the thinnest of threads, and Oren's heart broke for him all over again.

"Just a dream," he said gently. "Just your mind playing tricks on you."

They'd slept right through dinner and it was night out, he realized.

"Are you hungry? I can go to the cafeteria—"

Alex shook his head, tightening his grip. "No, *please.*"

"Okay," Oren said. He rubbed Alex's back, feeling the bumps of his spine and the curve of his ribs. "Not going anywhere, I promise."

Alex's trembling lessened, his body relaxing by increments, until his breathing was deep and even again and he was back asleep, face pressed against Oren's shoulder.

Oren fell asleep holding him, praying that he could keep him safe.

11

———

HE WAS ON A BEACH, the sand soft and gritty between his bare toes, the sun beating down on his head, warm breeze caressing his skin. Oren turned his face to the sunshine and drew a deep breath of salt-scented air.

"Took you long enough." The voice was achingly familiar, light and affectionate and amused, and Oren spun to see Ben lying in the sand, propped on his elbows.

Oren's heart clutched and he took a step closer. "Ben."

Ben smiled lazily at him, tipping his head back and exposing his long throat. "Where've you been, Orrie? I've been waiting for you."

"I—" Oren faltered. "Hiding, I guess."

Ben closed his eyes and dropped to his back, lacing his fingers across his flat belly. "You were always good at that."

Oren sat down next to him, unable to take his eyes off Ben's long body, sprawled unselfconsciously across the white sand, his skin golden as ever and the tiny blond hairs on his legs and arms curling and soft.

"I miss you," Oren whispered, his throat tight.

Ben turned his head to look at him. "I'm right here, aren't I? But you're not."

"Yes I am," Oren protested. "I *am* here."

Ben closed his eyes again and shook his head. "Nah, you're somewhere else. S'okay, Orrie. I always knew you'd leave me."

"I *didn't* leave you," Oren choked, his eyes stinging fiercely. "You left *me*, Ben, remember? You left, and I was all alone, and everyone hated me and I couldn't—I just couldn't. And now I don't know what to do."

Ben leaned forward and pressed their foreheads together. "Face the truth," he said, blue eyes holding Oren's from just a few inches away. "You know what it is. You just don't want to admit it."

OREN WOKE up with tears on his cheeks and Alex gripping his shoulder, shaking him gently.

"Please wake up," he was begging. "Oren, *please*."

Oren opened his eyes. Alex's face filled his vision, worry and fear writ large across his expressive features.

The pain from seeing Ben twisted in Oren's chest and he caught his breath on a sob. It was Alex's turn to gather him close, tucking Oren's head under his chin and crooning to him in Romanian.

Oren didn't let himself cry for long before he took a deep, gulping breath and sat up in the bed, wiping his eyes. "Sorry about that," he managed.

Alex sat up too, clearly still worried. "Is alright," he said, touching Oren's knee. "Was it… bad dream?"

"Looks like you're not the only one with unresolved issues," Oren said, sighing and scrubbing a hand through his hair. "What time is it?"

"Early," Alex said. "I need bathroom. Are you hungry?"

"I could eat," Oren admitted. He slid off the bed and handed the hospital crutches over so that Alex could maneuver his way to the bathroom under his own power. Oren waited outside the door until Alex came out, smiling at him as he slipped past and inside the small room.

When he was done, he came out to find Alex sitting cross-legged on the bed, his back straight and a very determined look on his face.

Oren blinked at him. "That's an expression that doesn't bode well for man nor beast."

"I do not know what that means," Alex said. "But you should go to cafeteria."

Oren's eyebrows climbed his forehead. "You sure about that?"

Alex firmed his mouth and nodded,

clutching his good ankle with both hands. "You will go… there and straight back, yes? Nowhere else?"

"Yeah," Oren said, closing the distance between them. Alex tipped his head back to look up at him, his throat working, and Oren cupped his face. "I'll be right back, I promise," he murmured, and bent to kiss him, soft and encouraging.

HE MADE it through the buffet line in record time, piling everything he could think of that Alex might like on the tray and then hurrying back up to the room, thankful that the orange juice was bottled so it didn't splash everywhere as he jogged down the hall.

Alex was in the same position, his eyes fixed rigidly on the door as Bethany fussed around him, taking his vitals. When Oren came in, Alex sagged, taking a deep breath, and managed a smile.

"Told you," Oren said cheerily. He saluted Bethany with a muffin from the tray and her lips quirked but she didn't answer, busy reading Alex's blood pressure.

"I got you blueberry, bran, and banana nut muffins," Oren said, putting the tray on the roll out table. "Also scrambled eggs, side of bacon, and some sausage. I'd make a joke about me liking sausage, but you probably wouldn't get it."

Alex snickered, ducking his head, and Oren gave him a delighted grin.

"I take it back, maybe you would! Dig in for me."

Alex chose a muffin at random and peeled the paper off, his long fingers quick and delicate. "You must eat too," he said, indicating the tray.

Oren picked up a piece of sausage and winked at him, making Alex laugh again, soft and charmed.

"You got that fever down, Mr. Costea," Bethany said as she removed the blood pressure cuff. "That's very good! Means you'll be able to leave today, as long as you promise to take care of yourself. No running on that ankle—in fact, no strenuous activity at all for the next few weeks. Take things slow and easy and don't push yourself too hard." She glanced at Oren. "You make sure of that."

"I will," Oren said quietly.

"Do you have somewhere to go?" Bethany asked. "It's not hospital policy to ask, but I'm worried about you two. Something weird's going on, that much is obvious."

Alex hunched his shoulders but Oren just smiled at her.

"We have somewhere to go, don't worry. We'll be fine, I promise."

THEY WERE out of the hospital by noon, blinking in the winter sunlight, Alex balancing on the crutches Bethany had given him.

Oren shoved his hands in his pockets, considering their options. "We can hitchhike to Cheyenne, but I think a bus is going to be our best bet. It'll take a little longer but we'll attract less attention."

Alex nodded silently and followed Oren down the block away from the hospital. Thankfully, the bus station wasn't far, just a few blocks over, but Oren was watching Alex uneasily by the time they got there. He was white, the dark circles under his eyes more pronounced again, and he swayed as Oren pulled the door open for him.

"Easy," Oren said, alarmed, and pointed at the hard plastic rows of seats. "You, sit. I'm going to buy our tickets. I'll be right there the whole time, okay?" He indicated the ticket counter, just a few yards away, and Alex nodded again, sprawling in one of the seats and dropping his crutches on the empty chairs beside him.

Oren bought their tickets and was relieved to hear that another bus was leaving within fifteen minutes and they'd just made it in time. He hurried back to Alex, who was sitting with his elbows braced on his knees, his head hanging.

"Hey," Oren said, scooting the crutches out of the way and sitting down beside him. "How are you feeling, donkey?"

Alex's mouth curved a fraction and he

leaned against Oren's shoulder. "Am alright. Just tired."

"Bus is leaving in fifteen minutes," Oren told him, rubbing his back. "You can rest once we're on it, maybe nap."

"*Bine*," Alex murmured.

They waited in silence until their bus was announced and then made their way aboard, Oren shepherding Alex ahead of him up the broad steps and down the aisle.

Alex chose seats at the very back and Oren stowed his crutches in the overhead compartment before sitting down next to him. The bus was almost empty, just a few other passengers closer to the driver, and they had the back to themselves.

Oren rubbed Alex's thigh and Alex tilted toward him again, putting his head down on Oren's shoulder.

"Where will we go?" he asked in a small voice.

"Once we get to Cheyenne?" Oren said. "Well, I've got a safe deposit box at a bank across town. It's got enough cash to keep us afloat until we're ready to tackle this properly, so I'll use it to get us clothes and food and toiletries and a motel room. The main thing that's holding us up is the marriage. We have to find someone willing to marry us, no questions asked, and that may take a day or three."

Alex lifted his head. "Mihai—"

"I know," Oren said. The bus rumbled out of the terminal in a cloud of smelly black smoke as he pulled Alex closer. "I'm doing everything as quickly as I can, but this *has* to be done first."

Alex sighed and put his head down again. "Thank you," he whispered, almost inaudible above the bus's engine.

"For you?" Oren said, keeping his voice light. "Any time, pal."

The trip took an hour and Alex slept almost the entire way, rousing as they hit the Cheyenne city limits and slowed down for a stoplight.

At the bus terminal, Oren found a bank of ancient payphones and called a taxi while Alex waited. When it arrived, he helped Alex into the warm, tobacco-scented interior and put his crutches in the trunk. Then he slid into the car himself, taking Alex's hand and leaning forward to address the driver.

"Wyoming Bank & Trust on Yellowstone Road, please." He sat back and squeezed Alex's hand as the taxi pulled away from the curb.

Oren paid the driver with the last of his cash. "This won't take long, you can keep the meter running," he said, and helped Alex out onto the pavement in front of the bank. Alex looked small and fragile in the pale green scrubs Bethany had given him, and he swallowed hard as Oren opened the door for him.

Inside, a friendly woman at the nearest desk greeted them and Oren pulled out his wallet, handing her a copy of his fake ID.

"I'd like to get into my deposit box," he told her with a warm smile.

"Of course, Mr. Alonzo," she said. "If you'll just follow me." At the vault, she pointed to a chair. "Your friend can wait there, if he likes."

Oren put his hand on Alex's shoulder and Alex looked at him, his eyes wide and worried. "I'll be right inside this room," Oren said, pointing. "Can you stay here? It won't take me a minute."

Alex swallowed again but nodded, sinking down to perch on the edge of the chair as Oren went inside the vault.

It took him less than a minute to clear out the contents and drop it all into the bag that was already in the box. When he came out, Alex was visibly tense, obviously pushed close to his mental limits.

"Come on," Oren said, pulling him to his feet. "Let's get you horizontal."

It was a testament to how exhausted Alex was that he didn't ask for clarification. He just stumbled out the door after Oren and back into the waiting taxi.

"Nearest decent motel," Oren told the driver.

They were pulling into a motel parking lot within five minutes and Oren gave the driver a hefty tip before bundling Alex out.

"Just a little further," he said, slipping an arm around his waist to steady him. "Do you want me to carry you?"

Alex shook his head, his eyes heavy, and Oren smiled at him, affection blooming warm in his chest.

"Donkey," he said, and Alex's lips twitched.

SAFELY IN THE MOTEL ROOM, Oren pointed Alex at the bed. "You. Sleep."

Alex balked. "But you—"

"I'll be right here," Oren said. "I won't leave without telling you. I will need to go get clothes and food for us at some point though, so would you rather I do that while you're asleep or awake?"

Alex's throat worked and Oren gave him a gentle push toward the bed.

"I—I do not—cannot I come with you?" Alex asked, sitting down on the edge of the bed and dropping his crutches.

Oren stepped between his knees, cradling his face in both hands as Alex tipped his head back to look up at him. "I wish you could, sweetheart, but it would attract too much attention. We're keeping this low profile, remember?"

Alex's lashes swept down and he leaned forward, pressing his cheek against Oren's stomach. Oren curled a hand around the nape of his neck, scraping his nails lightly against Alex's scalp.

"Can you do this?" he asked quietly.

Alex nodded against Oren's scrubs. "While I sleep," he said. "But will you... wait?"

"Until you're actually asleep?" Oren bent and took a quick kiss, soft like butterfly dust.

"Yeah, baby, I'll wait. Get yourself comfortable."

Alex obeyed, crawling under the covers and pulling his knees to his chest. Oren sat down next to him, resting a hand on his shoulder.

"You're safe," he said quietly. "Keep the door locked and don't open it for anyone, not even the maid. I'll be back as quick as I can."

"*Te iubesc*," Alex whispered, his eyes closed.

"One of these days you're going to tell me what that means," Oren said.

Alex smiled and tucked a hand under his cheek. "Perhaps."

OREN WAITED until Alex was asleep before he stood up, grabbed some cash from the bag, and tiptoed from the room, shutting the door soundlessly behind him.

He asked for directions from the desk manager and then walked briskly down the sidewalk in the direction of the nearest supermarket, where he got everything he thought he and Alex would need for the next several days.

An hour later, laden down with bags, he hurried back to the motel, careful not to slip on the wet pavement, the snow still melting. A sign caught his eye as he passed a small store and he hesitated and then ducked inside. *Two minutes,* he told himself. *I'll just ask, and if they don't have it, I'll go.*

When he fumbled the motel door open and staggered through, Alex was sitting up in bed, his arms around his knees, watching for him.

Oren kicked the door shut, dropped the bags and locked the door before crossing the room and crawling onto the bed.

"Look at you," he murmured, kissing Alex's cheek. "You're doing so well, sweetheart, I'm so proud of you."

Alex turned his head and caught Oren's mouth, straightening his legs and drawing Oren down on top of him.

Oren hummed, pleased with this development, and deepened the kiss, licking inside Alex's mouth as it opened for him.

They kissed for several long, leisurely moments, Alex's hands running up and down Oren's ribs and Oren bracing himself with an elbow on either side of Alex's head, but finally Oren broke away with a regretful sigh and sat up.

"I got you some clothes," he said. "Wanna see?"

Alex's eyes were dazed, but he nodded, pushing himself to a sitting position and crossing his legs as Oren hopped off the bed to rummage in the bags.

He pulled out a pair of soft jeans and held them up. "I had to guess at your inseam and waist, so try them on," he said. "If they don't fit, I'll take them back and get a different pair."

Next were several T-shirts, and then Oren lifted out a dark green sweater and tossed it over.

"I know it's not quite the same, but you seemed to like the one of mine that you were wearing… before," he said.

Alex felt the sleeve, his mouth working. "The color of Mihai's eyes," he whispered, looking up. "*Mulțumesc*, Oren."

Oren smiled at him, feeling that damn butterfly in his chest spreading its wings yet again. "Oh, I got you something else, too." He pulled out a copy of the book Alex had been reading and tossed it onto the bed next to him.

Alex picked it up, smoothing a hand across the cover. "Oren—"

"We're going to be stuck here for a couple of days," Oren said, sitting down on the bed beside him. "Figured you might like a way to pass the time."

Alex dropped the book and reached for him, pulling him down again. Oren laughed breathlessly against his mouth and rolled them so that Alex was balanced on top of him.

"Much better," he said, smiling up at him. "I'm a lot heavier than you—I don't want to squash you."

"You could not," Alex said, crossing his arms on Oren's chest and propping his chin on them. "I am much stronger than I look."

"I believe it," Oren said. He ran a gentle

thumb along Alex's cheekbone, exulting in the way Alex's lashes fell and he leaned into Oren's hand.

"I figure we'll call in for dinner, and I'll borrow the motel computer, do some digging for how to get married on short notice," Oren said after a few minutes. He smiled ruefully. "Not exactly something I've got much experience on. You can come with me, if you want, since I'm not leaving the motel itself."

"Yes please," Alex said instantly.

"Well, those clothes aren't going to try themselves on," Oren said. "Get hopping!"

Alex looked at him for a long minute and Oren just grinned until Alex sighed and leaned in for a kiss before rolling off and sitting up.

"So strange," he muttered, more to himself than to Oren.

THE JEANS FIT, Oren was delighted to see, a little too big in the waist but long enough, and Alex stuck out his good foot and wiggled his toes where they protruded from the denim cuff.

"I like them," he said, looking up with a wide smile.

Oren pushed the scrubs down and picked up his own pair of new pants, stepping into them and dragging them up over his hips. When he glanced up, Alex was watching him, eyes wide and dark, lips parted.

"What?" Oren said. "Is it my hair again?"

"I—no," Alex said. "Your hair is fine."

Oren narrowed his eyes but Alex just ducked his head and picked at a loose thread on his jeans, so Oren shrugged and pulled his scrubs top off. Bare from the waist up, he rooted through the bag until he found the shirt he wanted. When he straightened, Alex was watching him again, sneaking glances from under lowered lashes.

"Are you—are you checking me out?" Oren said.

"No!" Alex said, swiveling to put his back to Oren.

Oren swallowed delight and filed Alex's reactions away to examine properly when he had more time. "Ready to go?"

Alex bent and picked up his crutches and swung himself toward the door, where he waited, his eyes on the carpet, as Oren stepped into his shoes and closed the distance between them.

"You know what occurs to me," Oren said before he opened the door. "I don't think you and I have ever kissed standing up. We should remedy that."

Alex looked up and Oren tilted his head invitingly, taking a step forward, then another, until their bodies were flush together and Oren could slip his arms around Alex's narrow waist.

"What are you waiting for?" he murmured.

Alex's eyes darkened and he lowered his

head until their mouths met, sliding together warm and easy, like coming home or camping under Oren's favorite tree on summer nights, the stars wheeling above him in the endless skies and the breeze on his face.

When Alex lifted his head, Oren clung to him, disoriented.

"Goddamn, you're good at that," he managed after a minute.

"Only when I have good partner," Alex said, smiling at him.

Oren grinned back and reached for the door. "Let's go find ourselves a preacher."

12

It turned out that finding a preacher wasn't necessary. The county clerk would issue them a marriage license and marry them on the spot, no questions asked. The problem was going to be the legal documents required.

Oren turned to Alex, reading the page over his shoulder. "I don't suppose you have a passport."

Alex snorted.

"That's what I thought." Oren sighed and turned back to the screen. "Okay." He pulled up his email, which he checked about once a month, and composed a message.

While he waited for a reply, he looked at Alex, settled in the chair next to him, his long hands in his lap. Oren felt the by-now very familiar urge to smooth away the little furrow in Alex's brow, kiss a smile onto his lips and chase away the shadows, but Alex straightened.

"You have email," he said.

Oren glanced at the screen. "That was fast." He read the message and glanced at the time before hitting Reply. *ASAP*, he sent.

Less than a minute later, another message appeared. *Be here in an hour.*

Oren rubbed his hands together and closed the browser. "Hungry? We've got an hour to kill. I feel like pizza."

"You do not *look* like pizza," Alex said in tones of utter reason, and Oren nearly fell off his chair.

"Did you just—did you just make a bad joke at *me*?"

Alex ducked his head, a grin spreading across his mouth.

"Oh my God, I'm contagious," Oren said, laughing helplessly. "I've *corrupted* you."

THEY ORDERED a pizza and ate in the room, knees touching as they sat on the bed side by side. When it was time to go, Oren called for a taxi and they went down to the front to wait for it.

The cab dropped them off in front of a large apartment complex, water-stained brick with ivy desperately clinging to it where it hadn't been frozen off completely and weeds in the parking lot.

Alex looked uncertain but followed Oren inside the building and into the elevator for the seventh floor.

"Whatever happens, just roll with it," Oren said as the doors slid open and they stepped out into the dusty hall.

Alex's brow furrowed. "Roll… what?"

"Just… follow my lead," Oren said, and knocked on a door.

There was a loud thumping, a sudden yelp, and then quick footsteps pattering toward them before the door swung open and a pixie in a tank top scowled up at them.

"You're late," she snapped, flicking multi-colored dreads over one shoulder.

"No, we're not," Oren said reasonably. "You're just saying that to make me defensive and try to throw me off my game."

The girl studied him for a long minute and then grinned, bright flash of white in her dark face. "Can't blame a girl for trying," she said cheerfully. "Who's the hottie?"

"This is Alex," Oren said. "Alex, this is Anouk."

Anouk held out a sleek hand and Alex took it. "Nice to meet you," she said. "You are fine as fuck, anyone ever told you that?"

Alex slanted a look at Oren.

"I don't even go for men, but holy damn, you are easy on the eyes," Anouk said. "Are you single?"

Oren sighed and stepped between them as Alex started to look a little hunted. "Retract the claws, you know you're not actually making a pass at him so just knock it off already, would you?"

Anouk shrugged and spun, her neon hair

flying out in a bright nimbus around her head. "So you need papers, do you, Gorgeous?"

"Da," Alex said softly.

"Specifically, a passport and anything else we need to get legally married in the state of Wyoming," Oren said. "Something that will hold up."

Anouk spun back, gasping theatrically. "The famed bachelor, getting married at last? Say it isn't so!"

Oren fixed her with a look. "Do you think we could actually do what we came here to do?"

"Grumpy, jeez," Anouk muttered. She flopped into a folding chair in front of a bank of computers and began tapping keys. "Gonna need some information. Full name, birthdate, place of birth, personal number, things like that."

Alex didn't answer and Anouk pointed at him without looking.

"Talking to you, Hot Stuff."

"She's harmless, I swear," Oren murmured.

"Heard that," Anouk said.

Alex cleared his throat. "My name is Alex Costea. I was born in Vaslui, in Romania, the twelve of July, 1994."

Anouk perked up at that. "Romanian, huh? *Încântat de cunoștiință.*"

Oren watched in amazement as delight lit Alex's face and he turned toward Anouk like a flower opening to the sun, pouring out a flood of unintelligible words in his native tongue.

Anouk held up her hands, laughing. "Whoa, *whoa*. Way above my pay grade, pal. The only other thing I know how to say is *ţâţe faine.*"

Alex blinked and then dissolved into a fit of giggles, folding forward and wrapping his arms around his ribs as the mirth rolled through him. Oren just caught his crutches in time, bemused but enchanted at seeing Alex laughing so freely.

"What did you *say?*" he asked Anouk.

"Uh… nice tits," Anouk said, her grin widening. "Gotta have your priorities straight, man."

Oren snickered and cleared a nearby chair of its towering pile of books and papers, indicating that Alex should sit down. He did so as Anouk typed and Alex kept talking, giving her his parents' names and all the information he could.

"Do you have a personal number and do you know it if so?" Anouk asked, fingers still busy.

"Da," Alex said again, and reeled it off as she typed.

"Good," she said, flashing a distracted smile at him. "Okay, Cheekbones, need a picture of you. Stand up against that far wall for me."

Alex looked at Oren. "She is stranger than you," he said under his breath as he stood up, but there was still a faint smile in his eyes.

"Heard that too," Anouk sang.

Oren grinned at Alex and made sure he

had room to maneuver his crutches across the cluttered floor to the wall, where he straightened his shoulders, looking uncertain.

"Look this way," Anouk said, grabbing a camera. "Don't smile. Just stand there and be pretty, you can do that in your sleep."

Oren rolled his eyes. "Relentless," he mumbled. "Anouk, stop hitting on my fiancé. Alex, just look at the camera and ignore her."

Anouk clutched her chest. "No, help, it's too cute!" She put the camera on a tripod and fiddled with the controls, peering at the display. Finally she decided it was good enough and took several pictures, muttering to herself.

Oren pointed at the chair again. "You heard Bethany—gotta stay off that ankle."

Alex sat down, folding his hands in his lap as they waited.

It took awhile but eventually Anouk pronounced herself satisfied with the results. "It'll take me a few hours to put this together. Come back tomorrow morning and I'll have it ready then."

Oren kissed her cheek, making her laugh. "See you tomorrow."

He ushered Alex out of the apartment and to the elevator, where Alex leaned against the wall as it descended to the ground level. Oren looked at his face, concerned.

"Feeling okay?"

"Tired," Alex said, reaching for Oren's hand. "Tired of… being tired."

Oren stepped close, bracing Alex with his

shoulder. "You're recovering from a lot. You need to take it slow."

"I was runner, before," Alex said. "Fastest in village. No one could catch me. Now...." He lifted a shoulder.

"It'll come back," Oren said. The elevator dinged and they stepped out. The sun had gone down while they were with Anouk and there was a bite to the air. Alex shivered and Oren stopped and pulled his sweater off.

"No, you need it!" Alex protested. "I have mine, I am alright."

Oren just held it out, raising one eyebrow, until Alex sighed and took it, balancing awkwardly on one foot as he tugged it over his head.

"You fuss so much," Alex said, affection in his voice.

"Someone's got to," Oren said, and hailed a passing taxi.

BACK IN THEIR ROOM, they kicked off their shoes and settled on the bed. Oren pulled Alex against him, tucking him along his side, and picked up the remote.

"I wonder if there's anything interesting on," he mused.

He gasped with delight when he changed the channel and the television showed Fred Savage's baby face as he sat in bed, playing video games.

"Oh baby, you're in *luck*," he said. "Look, it's the best movie ever made!"

Alex looked doubtfully at the screen and back at him. Oren grinned.

"Trust me, you'll love it."

Oren privately thought there was nothing quite as much fun as introducing someone to a piece of his childhood and watching them fall head over heels in love with it just like he had, all those years ago.

Alex watched as Westley and Buttercup fell in love, braved the fireswamp, faced ROUSs, and when Billy Crystal waved the heroes off with a cheerful, "Have fun stormin' the castle!", Alex sat straight up.

"Oh," he said. "*Oh!*" He turned to see Oren grinning at him.

"Now do you get it?"

Alex laughed and lay down again, resting his head on Oren's shoulder. "You are still ridiculous," he said. "But you begin to make a little more sense."

Oren chuckled deep in his chest and rubbed Alex's back. He could feel the tension leaving his muscles as he relaxed, safe for the moment. *Safe forever, if I have anything to say about it*, he thought fiercely.

He waited for a commercial before he spoke. "Tomorrow, after we're married, we'll come back here and get our stuff, then I'll get the rest of my own affairs in order. Then we'll go to the police station with everything. I wish I'd thought to take pictures of the injuries you had when you showed up on my doorstep, but at least the hospital can verify them if necessary."

Alex had grown gradually tenser as Oren talked. He lifted his head, worry in his dark eyes. "Are you *sure*, Oren—"

Oren squeezed his arm, wordlessly rubbing reassuring circles into the skin. "We have to trust the cops to do their jobs," he said. "I promise, nothing will happen to Mihai."

Alex chewed on his lip, searching Oren's face, but finally he sighed and put his head down again. "Alright," he said, almost inaudible.

"Movie's almost over, and then you need to sleep," Oren said. "Tomorrow's going to be nuts."

Alex fell asleep just before the end, his long limbs draped over Oren's in an unself-conscious sprawl. He barely roused when Oren eased him over onto his side and slipped off the bed to go to the bathroom.

When Oren came back, he felt around in the bag from the bookstore until he came up with the other book he'd bought. A quick glance reassured him that Alex was still asleep, so Oren opened the book and scanned the pages until he found what he was looking for.

Then he stopped, stared at Alex for a long moment, and put the book back in the bag, tucking it away out of sight before climbing into the bed.

Alex stirred, murmuring something in Romanian, and squirmed back against Oren's warmth. Oren wrapped his arm around Alex's waist and pressed his face to the nape of his neck.

He fell asleep eventually, Alex a warm, trusting bundle in his arms.

13

THEY STOPPED at Anouk's apartment and picked up the passport first thing in the morning, both of them in neatly pressed button-down shirts and slacks.

Anouk took one look at them and wolf-whistled. "Looking *sharp*." She handed the burgundy passport to Alex with a flourishing bow, her neon dreads almost glowing as the morning sun hit them through the window.

Alex accepted it, smiling at her, and flipped through it as Oren leaned over his shoulder and made approving noises.

"Top shelf as ever," Oren told her as he handed over the cash.

Anouk preened. "Best in Wyoming, baby. Now get out of here, you two have a wedding to get to!" She all but shoved them out the door, flapping her hands at them like a tiny, vividly feathered bird, and winked at Alex as the elevator doors slid shut between them, cutting her off from view.

Alex slipped the passport into his pocket and took a deep breath.

"Are you ready to do this?" Oren asked quietly.

Alex nodded, firming his mouth. "Da. I am ready."

But he got more and more tense the closer their taxi got to the courthouse, and by the time Oren helped him out and inside the building, Alex was almost visibly jangling with nerves, his face white as a sheet.

Alarmed, Oren squeezed his shoulder. "Doing okay?"

Alex nodded silently, his lips pressed together, but he was trembling as he followed Oren down the hall to the county clerk's office.

He stopped a few feet from the door and Oren turned with his hand on the doorknob to see him wavering in the hall, his breathing rapid and his eyes wide as he shook his head.

"I—I cannot, Oren, I—"

Oren glanced around. They were alone in the hallway, but it was definitely not the place for a mental breakdown. To his left was an empty conference room, the lights off, and Oren shoved the door open and caught Alex's arm, pulling him inside.

Alex followed without resistance, his breath whistling in his lungs as he struggled to breathe.

Oren took his crutches and set them

against the wall, then eased Alex into a chair against the wall where they couldn't be seen from the hallway and knelt in front of him.

"Breathe for me, baby," he said, rubbing Alex's lean thighs. "You're okay, you're safe, everything's going to be okay."

Alex shook his head, gripping handfuls of his khakis until his knuckles turned white and dragging in air in great, gulping gasps.

"Is too much," he choked. "Too fast. You —will not want to be with me, after—" He squeezed his eyes shut, a tear leaking from the corner of one and sliding down his cheek. "I cannot be—" He clutched his hair, his frustration almost palpable.

"The marriage is happening too fast, is that what you're saying?" Oren said gently.

Alex nodded, swallowing a sob. "I am not… enough. You will regret—"

"Alex, honey, can you look at me?" Oren waited until Alex opened his eyes and met his gaze. "I was going to wait, maybe try and figure out how to say this properly, but I think you need to hear it now. See, I got a Romanian phrasebook when I bought your novel yesterday, and, um…." He took a steadying breath. "*Si eu te iubesc.*" He had a horrible feeling that he'd butchered the pronunciation, but it didn't seem to matter.

Alex had turned to stone, staring at him with his mouth open.

Oren rubbed the back of his neck, smiling at him. "That's what you've been saying to me, isn't it? That you love me?"

Alex covered his mouth and shook his head. "You cannot," he whispered, muffled against his palm. "Is too soon, too fast, and you should be with someone… like Ben. Not me, Oren, I am not—"

"I know it's fast," Oren interrupted. "I know you feel like you're falling off a cliff without a parachute right now, because that's how I feel too. But sometimes when it's right, you just *know*."

Alex sobbed out loud and covered his face with both hands. "What if you… change your mind?" he managed. "When you see—"

Oren touched his knee. "Listen to me, okay? It doesn't matter what's been done to you, what you've been forced to do to anyone else. That's not *you*. Alex, I killed the boy I loved when I was seventeen years old. Did that make me a bad person?"

Alex shook his head, dropping his hands to grab Oren's. "You are *best* person," he said, his voice still thick with tears.

"So are you," Oren said, smiling up at him as his eyes stung. "Can I—can I hold you?"

Alex made a helpless noise and tilted forward, sliding out of the chair into Oren's lap and clinging to him desperately.

Oren held on, rubbing his back. "Someday I'll get you to see how incredible you are," he whispered.

Alex's trembling began to ease after a few minutes and he lifted his head, blinking. There were tears on his cheeks, but his smile was genuine, soft like the unfolding of a butterfly's wing. His dark eyes were luminous in the dim room, wet lashes clumping together, and Oren caught his breath.

"God, you're beautiful," he whispered.

Alex ducked his head, pressing his face to Oren's shoulder. "*Mulțumesc.* So are you."

Oren huffed a laugh and rubbed Alex's back. "So what do you say, shall we get married?"

"Da," Alex whispered, pushing his face into Oren's chest a little harder. "Yes, Oren. Let's get married."

Oren helped him to his feet and held the door for him as Alex crutched his awkward way out into the hall and down the corridor to the county clerk's office.

A heavyset woman was sitting at the front desk and she glanced up as they entered. "Help you?" she said without much interest.

Oren cleared his throat. "We, uh… we'd like a marriage license."

The woman looked him up and down and Oren fought to keep from shifting his weight under her scrutiny.

"It's $125," she said after a minute. "Payable upfront. You wanting to get married here too?"

"If you're not too busy," Oren said, giving her his best winning smile, the one that Ben had always loved.

It seemed to have an effect on her too— her eyes softened and she almost smiled as she pointed at the two chairs in front of her desk.

"Sit. I'm Debora. What's your name,

honey?" This last was directed at Alex, who had stopped trembling but was still pale.

Oren settled Alex in the chair and sat down next to him.

"Alex Costea," Alex said, his voice almost inaudible.

Debora's eyes sharpened again and she leaned forward. "Alex, how old are you?"

Oren held his breath.

Alex lifted his chin. "Twenty-one."

"Got ID?"

Alex pulled his passport out and handed it over.

Debora's eyebrows went up. "Romanian? Don't see a lot of them in Cheyenne. And you're sure you want to marry this man?"

Alex nodded, taking Oren's hand. "So much."

Debora considered his face, but Alex's shoulders were back and his grip on Oren's hand was steady, and finally she nodded. "I'll need both your IDs, and you—" She pointed at Oren. "Start on these forms." She handed over a stack of papers and Oren gulped as he took it.

OREN WAS DEVELOPING a fine case of writer's cramps by the time he was done, but overall he thought he'd done a good job. Alex was reading over his shoulder, cheek pressed to Oren's shoulder blade.

"You spelled my name wrong," he said

suddenly, making Oren jump. "Is *Costea*, not Costa."

"Right, duh," Oren said, scribbling it out and fixing it.

Debora tapped her pen on the desk. "Okay, both of you sign it and put the date at the bottom." She waited until they were done and then stood, making a gesture for them to rise as well. "Raise your right hands, please."

Oren leaned in close to Alex. "Mawwiage is what bwings us togevver today," he said under his breath, and Alex's breath whooshed out of him in a startled, explosive laugh as his shoulders eased and he leaned against Oren's arm a little more.

"Do you, Alex Costea, take this man—" Debora squinted at the paper. "Orlando Acevedo, to be your lawfully wedded husband?"

Alex shot Oren a look and Oren shrugged.

"Alex?" Debora prompted.

"Sorry," Alex said, his attention snapping back to her. "Da, yes, I—sorry, how do I say?"

Debora smiled at him. "You can just say 'I do'."

"I do," Alex said instantly.

Oren swallowed hard as Debora turned to him and repeated the spiel.

"I do," he said as soon as she was done.

"I now pronounce you lawfully married in the state of Wyoming," Debora said. "You may kiss your husband."

Oren turned and pulled Alex close, Alex's body soft and yielding against him, and caught the back of his neck, tugging him down into a kiss. He could still taste the salt of Alex's earlier tears, but Alex's mouth was curving in a smile as he murmured something against Oren's lips.

When they broke apart, grinning foolishly at each other, Debora cleared her throat and handed Oren the marriage certificate.

"Congratulations," she said dryly.

THEY FOUND themselves on the sidewalk outside the courthouse somehow, Oren with no clear memory of how they got there. His head was spinning and all he could process was that he was *married* to Alex, that Alex was darting shy looks at him from under his lashes and clearly unable to fight his smile. Oren sympathized—his own face hurt from how widely he was grinning.

"What now?" Alex asked.

Oren tried to marshal his thoughts. "Now, we go back to the hotel and you rest, even if just for an hour. And then, we go to the police."

"No," Alex said. His jaw was set. "We go now. To the police."

"You're exhausted," Oren protested. "Who knows what's going to happen once we get there? You should rest first."

"No," Alex repeated. "Mihai, Oren. *Please.* We have to—"

Oren sighed. "Okay. You're right. I'm sorry."

Alex touched his face, fingers cold and soft. "You worry about me. But I worry about Mihai."

"Yeah. No, you're right. Let's go back to the hotel and get our stuff together and we'll go straight to the cops, okay?"

Alex's smile was brilliant. "Okay."

WHEN THE CAR ARRIVED, Alex climbed into the back of the cab and Oren handed his crutches in after him. As he straightened, he caught a glimpse of a black SUV cruising by, moving slowly on the slushy streets. Was it his imagination, or was it slowing down to get a look at him?

Not everyone is out to get you, he told himself, and slid into the cab, pulling the door shut behind him.

ALEX WAS CLEARLY MORE exhausted than he'd wanted to admit. He dropped his crutches and crawled onto the bed, curling up with his arms around his knees as Oren set the room to rights and packed their belongings.

When he was done straightening up, he sat down next to Alex, who rolled his head to look up at him silently.

Oren smoothed Alex's hair off his forehead. "It's going to be okay," he said.

"Do you have family?" Alex asked.

Thrown, Oren blinked. "I—yeah. My mom's back in Texas. I write to her when I can —I have to be careful, in case she's under surveillance, but after nearly a decade, I figure I'm not high on the priority list."

"What is… she like?"

"Flora Acevedo," Oren said, smiling. "She makes the best tortillas in the state of Texas. She'll make you some when you meet her, you'll see."

"Is she nice?"

"Got a mouth like a sailor and if you piss her off, you'll hear all about it," Oren said. Alex looked puzzled. "She swears a lot," Oren clarified. "But yeah, she's nice. She's the sweetest person in the world. You'll love her."

Alex swallowed. "Will you kiss me, Oren?"

"Considering that's just about my favorite thing to do, absolutely," Oren said, and bent to obey.

Alex's lips were soft and warm, parting beneath his, and he threaded a hand through Oren's hair, pulling him a little closer. He kissed along Oren's jaw, making him shiver, and down along his throat.

"*Te iubesc*," he whispered, lips feathery-soft on Oren's skin.

Someone knocked on the door. "Room service."

"We didn't order anything," Oren called, rubbing Alex's arm.

"Sorry, what?"

Oren grimaced. "Be right back," he told Alex, and slid off the bed.

He unlatched the door and it bounced inward violently, knocking him back. Thrown off-balance, Oren stumbled and went down, landing on his back, the impact driving the air from his lungs.

Alex screamed his name from the bed and Oren looked up at Nikolai's flattened face, grinning down at him, Mikhail leering over his shoulder.

"Remember me?" Nikolai said, and punched him.

14

Oren came to in stages, slipping in and out of consciousness, his awareness fragmented and faint. There were railroad spikes in his skull and red-hot pokers replacing several of his ribs, making it difficult to breathe. Something warm and heavy was pinning him in place, but he couldn't open his eyes, couldn't *see*—he made a huge effort and managed to pry one eyelid open.

He was staring up at an expanse of gray felt, a dome light in the center of it. *Backseat of a car*, his mind supplied. Oren turned his head, wincing as the movement drove the spikes deeper, to see Alex draped across him, his long limbs loose in unconsciousness, head hanging.

The vehicle went around a corner and hit the brakes hard, sending Oren and Alex in a wild sprawl onto the floor. Alex's elbow clipped Oren's cheek, snapping his head back, and Oren noted distantly that they hadn't bothered to tie Alex's hands.

His own hands were bound behind his back and he'd landed on something hard in his back pocket that was now digging painfully into his buttock. His little carving, the one he'd been making for Alex, he realized, and—

He squirmed, straining to reach his pocket as Alex lifted his head, a trickle of blood dripping from his nose onto his upper lip.

Oren. Alex's mouth shaped the word but he didn't speak.

"Be still," Oren whispered. Biting his lip so hard that copper burst bright and metallic on his tongue, he forced the fingers of his right hand into his pocket and closed them around his knife, feeling the silky curve of the bone handle in his palm as he pulled his hand back out.

He twisted sideways and pushed the knife into Alex's hand as the back door opened and a big hand came down, grabbing Oren by the back of the neck and hauling him from the vehicle with insulting ease.

Oren slid across the cold concrete, fetching up hard against a solid surface, arms wrenched painfully in their sockets.

Mikhail wasn't even looking at him. He'd turned back to the vehicle and was leaning inside. Alex's voice lifted and then there was a meaty thud, Mikhail's heavy fist cutting him off, and Alex made a muffled grunt as Mikhail dragged him out of the SUV.

Oren rolled onto his stomach, his head ringing, eyes unfocused, and struggled to push himself upright without the use of his hands. The driver's side door of the SUV opened and a pair of heavy boots appeared in his peripheral vision. *Nikolai*, Oren's brain supplied hazily.

Alex landed on the floor next to him, more blood dripping down his face from a fresh cut over his eyebrow.

"Sorry, Oren," he gasped. "So sorry, *dragă*. Mikhail, *no*—" as Mikhail reached down and caught Oren's collar, lifting him to his knees. Alex said something in Russian, clearly begging, and Mikhail laughed.

"You'll do that anyway, *syavka*," he said in his heavy accent.

Oren swayed, trying to catch his breath and take in his surroundings. They were in a garage, he thought, from what he could see through the eye that wasn't swollen shut. A door off to his left led into a richly paneled hall, warm light spilling through into the cold room they were in.

"Up," Mikhail said. He kicked Alex when he didn't immediately move and Oren made a noise that hurt his throat, struggling against his bonds.

"He can't *walk*, you bastard," he snarled.

Mikhail looked at Oren. "So you would carry him?"

"*Yes*," Oren said instantly. "Untie me, I'll carry him, *please*—"

Alex was shaking his head and Mikhail

laughed, the sound harsh and echoing in the cavernous space.

"Do I look stupid to you?"

Oren considered his options and decided the safest bet was to say nothing.

"I see you are not stupid either," Mikhail said. "On your feet." He nudged Alex with the toe of his boot. "Up, *syavka parshivaya*, or you will not like what happens next."

Nikolai had been leaning against the SUV, indolently examining his fingernails. He sighed, straightening. "Bring them inside," he said, stalking toward the door. "Andrei is not patient."

Alex got his hands underneath him, palms flat on the concrete, and pushed himself up, balancing awkwardly on his good foot. He said something else in Russian, his voice like ground glass, harsh and pleading.

"*Nyet*," Mikhail said. He bent and hauled Oren upright by one arm, and Oren just managed to stifle a scream as his abused arm protested the movement. "Inside," Mikhail said, giving him a rough shove toward the door. "Andrei wants to see you."

Oren balked, turning to look at Alex, arms wrapped around his ribs and shoulders hunched, looking small and defenseless as he swayed in place.

Mikhail pushed him again and Oren stumbled forward, not taking his eyes off Alex, who looked back dumbly, blood and tears streaking his face. Mikhail turned and swung

Alex up over his shoulder, easier than hefting a bag of flour.

He jerked his chin at Oren and Oren got the message and limped through the door into the hall.

It was warm in the house, lights glowing with a mockery of welcome, the soft carpet muffling their footfalls. The hall stretched out ahead of him, doors lining one side and a set of stairs at the far end.

"Third floor," Mikhail said from behind him, giving him another shove, and Oren tensed. "Oh, try it, *suka*," Mikhail said, wicked delight in his voice.

Oren sagged. Even with Alex over his shoulder, Mikhail could wipe the floor with him and they both knew it.

He climbed the stairs with dragging feet, dreading what was coming. Mikhail was right behind him, giving him a helpful jab every time Oren slowed down too much.

Finally the stairs ended, and Oren found himself on a carpeted landing with a door in front of him. Mikhail reached around him and opened it, shoving Oren through and it took him a minute to orient himself and figure out what he was seeing.

Banks of monitors lined two walls, showing the insides of small, dingy rooms. Some were empty. Others... Oren swallowed nausea.

A girl sat on the edge of her bed, head bowed, the bumps of her spine clearly visible even on the grainy video feed, despair in every line of her body. As Oren watched, the door swung open and a man stepped inside.

Mikhail kicked the back of Oren's knee, buckling his legs and dropping him to the floor in a graceless sprawl. He shrugged Alex off his shoulder to fall next to Oren and then stepped back, out of sight behind them.

Oren was on his side, unable to sit up with his hands bound behind him. Alex's breath was coming in sharp, short puffs, his eyes wide and glassy, and Oren tried to smile at him. Alex didn't seem to register it.

"Oh, untie him." Andrei's voice was as sleek and deadly as Oren remembered. "He's about as dangerous as a kitten."

This kitten will tear out your throat with its teeth, Oren thought, but he kept his mouth shut as Nikolai's boots appeared in front of him and cold metal kissed his wrists as Nikolai's blade sliced through the rope.

As soon as he was free, Oren reached for Alex and pulled him into his arms.

Andrei hummed, sounding touched. "So sweet," he murmured. "Misha, go back to the hotel. Make it look like they left in a hurry, but no signs of foul play, you understand?"

"Da," Mikhail muttered, and his heavy boots thumped on the soft carpet as he left the room.

Nikolai stepped back, leaning one shoulder against the wall as he cleaned his fingernails with the tip of his knife. Andrei was sitting in a comfortable chair in front of the banks of monitors, his long legs sprawled out in front of him, arms slung behind his head in indolent comfort.

He smiled, a baring of teeth, and fear rippled through Oren in a sluggish, curling wave. "It would appear you lied to me, Mr. Asher."

"I lie to most people," Oren said, lifting his chin. "Don't take it personally."

"Ah, the kitten has claws!" Andrei said, and his smile widened. "You took something that belongs to me. I want it back."

Alex hadn't made a sound, clinging to Oren like he was drowning, head down so he couldn't see Andrei's face.

Oren glanced at Nikolai, who hadn't moved, and back at Andrei. "Dunno what you're talking about."

"Don't be tedious," Andrei said. He sat up and Alex flinched backward. "You took my whore, and my whore took a very important thumb drive. So give them both back and I'll consider letting you walk out of here with both your legs."

"Alex doesn't belong to you," Oren hissed, fury tightening his voice. "He's his own person."

Andrei rolled his eyes, collapsing back against his chair cushion. "I have neither the time nor patience to explain how wrong you are." His next words were directed at Alex. "Where is it, *syavka*? Tell me, and I'll let this *suka* go."

Alex took a deep breath and lifted his head a fraction, but Oren spoke before he could.

"All we want is Mihai," he said. "We'll make you a trade—Mihai for the thumb drive. You let us walk, we give you the drive, everyone's happy."

"That's all you want?" Andrei mused. "That's all. You want two of my top earning whores to walk out of here in good health, when they still have so much potential?"

"You call *that* good health?" Oren spat, gesturing at Alex's bony frame.

"He can still fuck, it's good enough," Andrei said dismissively, and Oren tightened his grip on Alex to keep from lunging at him and getting them both killed.

"I'll tell you where it is," Alex said suddenly, lifting his head.

"Finally, we're getting somewhere." Andrei stretched his legs out and gestured for Alex to continue.

"Promise me you'll let Oren go without hurting him. *Promise.*" Alex's voice cracked like a whip, and Andrei raised a lazy eyebrow.

"Alex, no—" Oren started, but Andrei spoke over him.

"*If* the contents of the drive are undisturbed, I'll consider it."

"They are," Alex said. "You have to promise."

Andrei lunged forward almost out of his seat and Alex cowered backward into Oren's frame. "*You* don't fucking tell me what to do, *syavka*," Andrei hissed. "I said I'll consider it. That's as good as you're getting. Now tell me where it is."

Oren could feel Alex's trembling, but he managed to lift his chin.

"I want to see Mihai first."

"You are growing tiresome," Andrei snarled, but he flicked a finger at Nikolai, who turned and left the room.

Alex's trembling was getting worse, his fingers clutching at Oren's arm hard enough to bruise.

"Just hang on," Oren whispered against his hair.

The door banged open and Nikolai flung a thin young man through, hard enough he lost his balance and fell in a windmill of skinny limbs.

"*Mihai!*" Alex tore himself from Oren's embrace and scrambled on his knees across the dirty carpet to fling his arms around Mihai, who clutched him back just as desperately.

A flood of angry-sounding Romanian poured from Mihai, and Alex shook his head, replying in kind as Mihai shoved at him, clearly furious.

"Aw, just now reunited and already squabbling?" Andrei said. He crossed his feet at the ankle and grinned conspiratorially at Oren, who didn't return it. "Siblings, eh?"

Mihai choked on a sob and wrapped his arms around Alex's neck, burying his face in his shoulder. Tears poured down Alex's face and he glanced back at Oren briefly, then closed his eyes and pressed his cheek to the top of Mihai's head.

"Enough of this touching reunion," Andrei announced. "Alex, the drive. Now."

"L-let Oren go," Alex managed.

Andrei moved with the speed of a striking snake, grabbing Alex's hair and wrenching his head back. Oren tensed and Nikolai shook his head at him.

"What did I say about telling me what to fucking do?" Andrei hissed in Alex's ear. "You need a reminder of your lessons, is that it?"

"Please," Mihai said, pulling on Andrei's wrist. "Please don't hurt him, *please*—"

Andrei shook him off as if he didn't even register Mihai's weight.

"Tell me, and maybe your *suka* lives," he said to Alex. "Do you really want his death on your conscience?"

Alex's head was immobilized, but he cut his eyes toward Oren, halfway to his feet across the room, and his throat worked. "Downstairs," he husked.

"What?" Andrei demanded.

"Downstairs," Alex repeated, a little louder. "In... garage, behind paint cans."

"You hid it in my own house," Andrei said incredulously. "You left it... *here*? This whole time?"

Alex closed his eyes, still dangling from Andrei's hand.

Andrei jerked his chin toward the door and Nikolai left on soundless feet as Andrei let go. Alex slid bonelessly to the floor and curled in a ball, arms back over his head, Mihai curving his body over his in a desperate attempt to shield him, and Oren felt hot tears leaking down his face. He gathered himself, getting to his knees, as Nikolai left the room and shut the door behind him.

OREN CRAWLED across the carpet and put his arm around Alex's thin shoulders, pressing his cheek to Alex's hair. Mihai didn't lift his head, still clinging to Alex like he could protect him by sheer force of will.

"Okay," Oren whispered. "Hold on, baby."

"Do you know what I find most incredible?" Andrei asked, and Oren shot him a poisonous look.

Andrei didn't seem to notice. "Alex got away. The whimpering *syavka* actually escaped. He could have run. There for a while, I thought he was dead, or at least hoped he was. He could have made a life for himself somewhere else. But instead, he came back. Walked right back into the lion's den and gave himself up for his sniveling little brother, as if him being here makes the *slightest* bit of difference, as if he can somehow make Mihai's life better?" He laughed. "He's a *whore*. They're *both* whores. And he chose that, all to be near family. Honestly, it's pathetic."

Oren surged to his feet, clenching his fists. The room tilted around him as his head protested the sudden movement, but he gritted his teeth and ignored it. "I'm going to kill you," he rasped, and charged.

Andrei sidestepped neatly, catching Oren by the back of his shirt and using his momentum to fling him against the wall.

Oren got his hands up just in time to stop his head from hitting the drywall as a sickening *crack* shivered through his wrist. He landed with a thud, gasping for air around the pain that was suffocating him, and Andrei loomed above him.

"You are as stupid as you are noble," he snarled. "Did you really think I would let you *or* the *syavka* live, after what you did? Did you really think you would walk away from this?" He fumbled in his coat pocket and dread turned Oren to ice as Andrei pulled out a small, snub-nosed pistol. "I was going to do this outside, where you wouldn't stain the carpets with your blood, but—" Andrei shrugged again. "I can always replace the carpet." He pointed the gun and squeezed the trigger. Oren flung his arms over his head, curling in on himself, knowing it was futile. The shot was deafening in the confines of the room, and then there was silence.

Oren lowered his arm. There was a hole in the wall just above his head. Oren turned to see Andrei crumpling to the floor, his throat a bloody ruin, blank shock in his eyes. When he fell, Alex was standing behind him, the blade in his hand dripping crimson.

"The knife knew where to go," he whispered, and collapsed.

15

 OREN FLUNG HIMSELF OVER ANDREI, slipping in the blood, and pulled Alex and Mihai across the room, away from the body. Alex was limp and unresisting in his arms, head lolling, and Oren laid him flat on the floor, listening for his heartbeat and nearly crying with relief when he heard it.

"Alex," Mihai pleaded, patting Alex's cheek. "Wake up, Alex, we have to go, wake up—"

Oren closed his eyes, resting his forehead on Alex's chest. Mihai was right, they had to go, had to escape before Nikolai came back. For that matter, why hadn't the gunshot brought him running? Oren took a deep breath and stood up. Mihai watched him, eyes unsure, as the room tilted and swayed again and Oren gritted his teeth. *Not the time.* He tiptoed to the door and eased it open a crack. There were shouts from downstairs, the sound of running feet echoing up the stairwell. Oren glanced over his shoulder at the monitors and his mouth fell open in shock.

Uniformed police officers were pouring into each room—in some, men in various stages of undress were spread-eagled on the floor, and in others, the officers were talking to the prostitutes who'd been alone in their rooms.

"Alex," Oren said, stumbling across the room and going to his knees with a thump. "Alex, honey, wake up, the cavalry is here."

"Who *are* you?" Mihai demanded.

Alex's eyes fluttered and Oren patted his cheek.

"Come on, baby, wake up for me. We need to go downstairs."

Alex opened his eyes and Oren smiled at him, a lump in his throat.

"Hey there, hero. Can you sit up?"

Alex looked at Mihai, then swallowed and nodded, accepting Oren's hand and allowing him to pull him to a sitting position and then to his feet.

They went down the stairs carefully, Alex's arms around Oren's and Mihai's shoulders. On the second floor landing, they were enveloped in a swirl of chaos, loud voices and heavy boots, commands for them to show their hands, and Oren obeyed, giving them both a nod to comply as well.

"My name is Orlando Acevedo," Oren said clearly. "I'm turning myself in. This is my husband, Alex Acevedo, and his brother, Mihai Costea."

"Your *what?*" Mihai demanded.

A SWAT officer approached, rifle pointed at Oren's chest. "On the ground," the man said. "Facedown, all of you. No sudden movements."

"Alex has a broken ankle," Oren said as they went to their knees. "Please be careful with him. Oh, also, there's a dead body upstairs."

16

───────

ALEX AND OREN were separated almost immediately, and the last Oren saw of him, Alex was looking over his shoulder at him, his eyes wide and terrified as a young female officer led him away with Mihai, speaking soothingly to them.

Oren was escorted out of the house to a waiting ambulance and seated in the back where a paramedic could treat his injuries while a detective spoke to him.

He was finding it hard to focus, his vision and hearing fuzzing in and out. He thought the detective had said her name was Nguyen, but he couldn't be sure.

"I want to see my husband," he said when the detective had stopped talking.

Detective Nguyen glanced over her shoulder, presumably to where Alex was being tended. "The paramedics are taking care of him," she said. She had kind eyes, Oren thought absently. "We'll let you see him as soon as possible, but right now I need to know your version of events."

"How did you guys even know where we were?" Oren asked. "We didn't call you—we were going to, but they grabbed us before we could."

Detective Nguyen smiled. She was wearing an astonishingly ugly plaid jacket, with shoulder pads and boxy pockets, and it dwarfed her small frame. "We got an anonymous tip that someone was being attacked. When we pulled up, the garage was open and there was blood on the floor, which gave us the probable cause we've been looking for to enter the premises and shut this place down."

"You knew about Andrei," Oren said numbly.

Detective Nguyen lifted a shoulder, her mouth twisting. "We had no solid leads. Andrei is—*was*—smart. And ruthless, as I think you know by now. He buried any evidence that might have damned him, and every witness we lined up against him either went missing or mysteriously forgot what had happened when it came time to testify." She leaned forward, eyes serious. "Between you and me, Mr. Acevedo, you're a hero. You did what the law would not allow us to do."

"I just wanted to keep Alex safe," Oren whispered, clutching the blanket around his shoulders a little closer. "And... Mihai." He closed his eyes as tears prickled.

"Can you tell me what happened?"

"It's... a long story," Oren said. His head was throbbing and it was entirely possible he was floating.

"Start with the events of today," Detective Nguyen suggested. "I'll get the rest of it later, once you're feeling a little better."

"We got married," Oren said. "This morning." It felt like a lifetime ago, an entirely separate reality. "We were at the hotel. In... bed." He shot a look at Nguyen, but she just nodded for him to continue. "Someone knocked, I thought it was room service. It wasn't."

He took the detective through everything that had happened until Andrei pulled his gun out, and then hesitated.

"I need to know everything," Nguyen said, her voice suddenly steely. "Don't try to protect anyone. Tell me exactly what went down."

Oren closed his eyes. "Andrei tried to shoot me. He... missed. I think I had my arms over my head—it all happened so fast. When I looked, Andrei was dead and Alex...." He swallowed. "Alex was holding my knife." He reached for Detective Nguyen's sleeve. "He did it to protect me," he said urgently. "He saved my life, Detective, we'd both be dead right now if he hadn't—"

Detective Nguyen gently disentangled herself, patting Oren's hand. "I think that's all I need right now. Thank you for your honesty, Mr. Acevedo."

"Lie down," the paramedic said. "You've

got a hell of a concussion and you need to rest."

Oren obeyed, sinking back against the gurney and letting the chaos spin on around him.

OREN WOKE up in a hospital bed, feeling much clearer-headed, a cast on his left wrist, dismayed but not surprised to see that he was handcuffed to the bed. He pressed the call button and a nurse and a uniformed officer entered.

"I want to see my husband," Oren told the nurse, whose nametag said SELENE.

Selene glanced at the officer, big and stone-faced beside her. He hesitated and then turned away to speak into his radio. When he turned back, he shook his head.

"He's sedated."

"I need to talk to him," Oren insisted. "Please, I need to know he's okay."

"He's *sedated*," the officer said. "Out cold." Selene made an irritated noise and the officer shot her a guilty look, hesitating. "I'll ask if you can see him as soon as he comes around."

SEVERAL HOURS PASSED and Oren tried in vain to think about anything but Alex with the knife in his hand, his face empty as he stood over Andrei's body.

Finally, Selene came back in the room and Oren looked up.

"Can I see him?"

"He's awake," Selene said. "He's... not talking. Detective Nguyen asked me to bring you down there, see if you can help."

Oren threw the covers off, swinging his legs out of the bed. He was brought up short by the handcuffs and he looked at Selene.

"Stay there," Selene said. "I'll take the bed down to Alex's room."

Oren settled back against the mattress as Selene got the bed ready to move and then wheeled him out into the hall and past several doors.

Alex was sitting up in bed, Mihai in the bed beside him. Alex was holding Mihai's hand, their beds pushed together, but his head was down, eyes fixed on the door. Detective Nguyen was next to him, asking a question in a gentle voice, when Selene pushed the door open and Alex sat up straight.

Oren managed a smile, even though he wanted to cry at the bruised shadows under Alex's eyes, the way he twitched at the slightest noise and held Oren's gaze like it was the only thing keeping him from drowning. "Hey, *catâr*," Oren said around the lump in his throat, and Alex's mouth twisted but he said nothing, watching Oren with an almost unnerving intensity.

Selene pushed the beds together and Oren reached for Alex, swearing under his breath when the cuff pulled him up short again. He looked at Detective Nguyen, who'd been observing them silently, and held up his wrist.

"Please," he said. "Post a guard outside the room or *in* the room, I don't care, but *please*. I need—" He swallowed hard. "He needs me to hold him."

Detective Nguyen looked at Alex, at the way he was leaning toward Oren like filings drawn to a magnet, and finally sighed, pulling her keys from her pocket. She unlocked Alex's cuff first—*where was he even going to go on a broken ankle?* Oren wondered—as Alex shrank from her touch, his eyes still fixed on Oren. Then she leaned over and took Oren's manacle off and stepped back.

Oren reached out as Alex nearly fell across the beds toward him. He burrowed into Oren's chest, clinging with a desperate strength as Oren rubbed his back, resting his cheek against Alex's silky hair.

"Okay," he whispered. "I'm okay, see? I'm here. Everything's okay. Look, Mihai's here too. It's all okay now, just like I told you it would be."

Detective Nguyen turned away, looking out the window to give them a moment of privacy. The coat was just as ugly under fluorescent lighting, Oren noted. Mihai didn't turn away, watching Oren holding Alex with an unnerving intensity on his thin face, but he said nothing.

After a few minutes, Oren eased away. There were tears on Alex's face, but he still hadn't made a sound. Oren wiped one away with his thumb and Alex leaned into his touch.

"Feel like talking?" Oren murmured.

Alex's face shuttered and he pressed closer.

"I know, sweetheart," Oren said, keeping his voice light. "But I have a feeling that Detective Nguyen, she of the pretty brown eyes and the really hideous jacket over there, isn't going to go anywhere until you talk to her."

Nguyen sputtered but Alex's taut frame eased and he let out a quiet sigh.

Oren winked at Nguyen over the top of Alex's head. "He thinks I'm strange because I make weird jokes."

Nguyen's mouth curved and she settled back on her heels.

"Alex?" Oren said gently. He held up a finger, hoping Nguyen would follow his lead. *Wait.*

Nguyen hesitated but she kept her mouth shut.

Alex was still for a long moment and then he tilted his face up, asking wordlessly, a plea in his eyes. Oren cradled his jaw, fingers brushing the curls at Alex's nape, and slotted their mouths together.

I'm here, he told Alex silently as they kissed. *I'm with you. You're safe.*

Alex's lips were salty but his mouth was sweet, yielding and soft beneath Oren's. When they broke apart, Alex sat up in the bed and turned to face Detective Nguyen.

"My name is Alexandru Costea," he said. Oren scooted closer, wrapping an arm around Alex's waist and bracing him with his presence as Alex continued. "My brother—" He broke off to look at Mihai, and Oren pressed a kiss to his shoulder. "My brother Mihai and I were whores... for Andrei Sokolova." Alex took a deep breath. "I killed him. Andrei."

"There's a *whole* lot more to the story than that," Oren said before Detective Nguyen could speak. "Maybe start with the night you escaped? His English isn't great," he continued, addressing Nguyen, "so please be patient."

Nguyen just nodded as she pulled up a chair and opened a notebook to start taking notes.

Alex began to speak, his voice low and halting. Oren kept silent, only speaking up to offer a word when Alex floundered.

It took awhile, especially in Alex's faltering English, but he took them through the harrowing details of his escape, and Oren felt tears sliding down his own face as Alex recounted how Mihai had pushed him out the window and told him to run even as Andrei had loomed over him.

"I saw—" Alex gulped for air. "Andrei behind him—he grabbed him—"

"I fought," Mihai said to Detective Nguyen, speaking for the first time. "I never —I never fought before. Alex, he always fought for me." He turned to Alex. "But I fought him, Sandu, I fought him so hard, I

slowed him down so you could get away—"
His voice was thick with tears and Alex said
something in Romanian to him. Mihai
choked on a laughing sob and covered his
mouth with his free hand.

"Take your time, Alex," Detective Nguyen
said. Her eyes were sympathetic, her posture
relaxed and unthreatening, and Alex nodded,
gulping air.

"I... ran," he whispered. "I did not know...
where. I just... ran. I saw...." He leaned into
Oren's chest. "I saw Oren's house. I thought
—maybe I can steal food. I was so hungry.
But I was cold and so tired, I pass out, and—I
wake up and Oren was there, he—help me.
He saved me."

"I helped a little," Oren corrected. "You
did most of this yourself, sweetheart."

Alex heaved a shuddering sigh, relaxing a
little. He began to speak again, telling the
detective of the time they'd spent snowed in
together—*the week we fell in love*, Oren
thought—and their flight from Andrei's men.

"They burned your house down, Mr.
Acevedo?" Nguyen said.

Oren nodded. "They'd just been shooting
at us and we were running at the time, I
didn't stop to watch them light the match,
but... yeah."

Detective Nguyen listened keenly as Alex
resumed his tale, the hospital in Laramie and
then coming back to Cheyenne, getting
married, preparing to go to the police with
their story.

"And then Andrei found you?" Nguyen asked.

Alex nodded. "Oren is... artist. He carves beautiful things. He give me... his knife. Andrei tried to shoot Oren, and I—" He took a deep breath. "I stop him." He met Nguyen's eyes. "I kill him. I would do it again."

Detective Nguyen's lips twitched. "Maybe keep that last fact to yourself," she said dryly.

"What happens now?" Oren asked.

"Alex needs to rest," Nguyen said, standing up. "Mr. Acevedo, I need to speak to you alone."

"I'll be right back," Oren told Alex.

Alex squared his shoulders and nodded.

Oren followed Nguyen out into the hallway, where she turned to face him.

"You're going to be extradited to Texas," she told him bluntly.

Oren rubbed the back of his neck. "I assumed as much," he admitted. "What about Alex?"

Detective Nguyen opened her mouth and was cut off by a voice down the hall.

"Detective Nguyen! Bob Clark, Cheyenne Daily News, can I get a quote from you?"

Oren and Nguyen spun to see a balding, portly man in his forties panting toward them, a cameraman with a huge camera and boom mike right behind him.

"*Fuck*," Nguyen muttered. "The chief of police will be addressing the media later this afternoon, after I've briefed him, Bob. No statements now."

Bob swiveled to look at Oren. "Are you Oren Asher?" he asked.

Oren froze. "I—uh… how do you know my name?"

"You *are*! Mr. Asher, can you give me a brief comment about how you and Alex Costea fell in love? How did you meet? What went down in that house? You're a hero, did you know that?"

"That's it, we're done," Nguyen snapped, and hustled Oren back into the room.

"How the fuck did he know all that?" Oren demanded as Nguyen pointed at the bed. He climbed back into it and she cuffed him to the railing again, not looking at him.

Alex was sitting up, worry all over his expressive face. "Oren?"

Oren smiled at him. "It's okay, honey. Detective?"

Nguyen blew out an explosive breath, ruffling her heavy bangs. "Fuck it, you're going to hear sooner or later. Someone called every major news station in town, as well as most of the minor ones—I'm betting it's the same anonymous tipper who called us in the first place—and spun them a fairytale about the two of you meeting and falling in love and you, Oren, riding in on your white horse to save the day and stop the villain. The press is eating it *up*. You're on every news broadcast in the city. Damn thing's going viral."

"That's not how it happened, though," Oren protested, taking Alex's hand. "I mean… yeah, we fell in love and everything, but there was no white horse, I'm not even the one who stopped Andrei—that was all Alex."

"They don't care," Nguyen said, shrugging. "It's *romantic*." Mihai made a noise of disgust as Nguyen leveled a look at Oren. "You need to go back to your room."

"*No*," Alex said, his grip tightening on Oren's hand to the point of pain. "Please, please no, Oren, I cannot—" His breathing shortened as his face whitened and Oren swore, leaning over the bed to try and catch Alex's eyes.

"Baby, breathe for me. Look at my face, it's okay, I'm right here. Look, Mihai's here too. See? We're both here, you're okay. In and out, there you go, slow and deep." He smiled as Alex held desperately to his hand, watching his face. "You're doing so well, *catâr*."

"What does that mean?" Nguyen asked, and Alex flinched at the sound of her voice.

"It means donkey," Oren said, "because he's a stubborn ass. Detective, please—don't separate us. He just went through a horribly traumatic event, and he had separation issues even before what happened today. Please, if you're human under that plaid monstrosity, give him a break."

"What the fuck is wrong with this jacket?" Nguyen complained.

"We've all three given our statements," Oren pointed out. "It's not like we're going to collaborate on some fabricated retelling of events or something."

Nguyen pursed her lips, studying them.

Finally she sighed. "God, I'm getting as soppy as Mel. Who, by the way, is going to laugh her ass off when she hears about this." She pointed at Oren. "Keep him quiet so the nurses don't have to sedate him. We *will* need to speak to him again."

"Who's Mel?" Oren asked.

Nguyen flashed him a smile, transforming her face as she headed for the door. "My partner. In every sense of the word."

THE ROOM WAS quiet after Nguyen left, and Oren turned on his side so he could see Alex's face as Alex did the same. Mihai was silent, but when Oren glanced over, he was watching them, reservation in his eyes.

Oren sighed and sat up again. "Hey, uh… Mihai. We haven't been properly introduced. I'm—"

"I know who you are," Mihai interrupted. "You make my brother think he's in love with you."

"*Mihai!*" Alex protested, struggling to sit up. He said something in Romanian, anguish in his voice, and Mihai's lip curled. He was still staring at Oren as he bit off something in reply and Alex flinched like he'd been hit.

"Hey, *whoa*," Oren said, putting out a hand. "Whatever you just said, no more of that. Do you have any idea what Alex went through to get you back?"

Mihai sneered at him. "He's my brother," he snarled. "You don't come between us."

"I'm not *going* to come between you or take him from you," Oren said, keeping his voice even with an effort. "That's the last thing I want to do."

"He loves me more," Mihai spat. "He'll always love me more."

"Is not contest!" Alex cut in. "Mihai, I love *both*. I can love both." He switched into Romanian again and whatever he said made Mihai flinch and pluck at his blanket with his thin fingers. He replied, sounding chastened, and Alex's response was softer too.

Oren let go of Alex's hand, some vague thought of making Mihai feel less threatened driving him, but Alex shot him a challenging look and recaptured it, squeezing fiercely. Oren sighed and squeezed back.

Mihai's mouth tightened, but Alex said something sharp, and he scowled, crossing his arms.

"You should lie down," Oren said to Alex, who nodded and repositioned himself.

Mindful of Mihai's judgmental gaze, Oren lay down with a careful foot of space between them. From the look Alex gave him, it didn't go unnoticed, but he didn't comment on it.

"Go to sleep, Mihai," Alex said, in English for Oren's benefit.

Mihai muttered something but then there was silence.

Alex scooted an inch closer, and Oren smiled at him.

"Hey," he whispered.

The shadows behind Alex's eyes lightened a fraction. "*Te iubesc*, Oren."

"I love you too, donkey," Oren murmured. "Try to sleep, okay? You're still recovering and you've had a *very* bad day."

Alex nodded and after a few minutes, his eyelids began to droop. It wasn't long before he was asleep, as Oren held his hand and drifted to sleep himself.

A NURSE CAME and checked their vitals and Oren dozed through it, only half-aware, knowing only that Alex was still asleep and there was no cause for alarm.

SOMEONE TOUCHED his ankle and Oren jerked his head up, startled. Alex stirred and squirmed a little closer, murmuring something in his sleep as he slung an arm over Oren's waist. Oren looked toward the end of the bed.

A young woman was standing there, smiling at him. Mihai was still asleep in the opposite bed. Oren blinked.

"You're not a nurse."

"Nope," she said, keeping her voice low. "I'm Meera. Friend of Anouk's."

Oren sat up straight, a hand on Alex's shoulder. "What are you doing here?"

Meera winked at him. She was Indian,

long black hair in braids pulled up in a messy bun on top of her head, a slim gold ring in her nostril reflecting the light. Her dark eyes were bright and inquisitive, and when she turned her head to check that the door was closed, Oren caught a glimpse of a golden and red dragon tattoo twining up her neck.

"I run one of the highest rated blogs in the city," Meera said, turning back to him. "I cover breaking news, social injustice, and celebrity gossip." Oren stared and she shrugged. "People like it, and it makes enough ratings that I can keep covering stories that mean a lot to me."

She turned and pulled a chair over to the side of the bed, sitting down and folding her hands in her lap. "Anouk said you'll give me an exclusive."

"She did, did she," Oren said flatly. Alex stirred again, his arm tightening around Oren's waist as he lifted his head and blinked. Oren could feel the tension that snaked through his body when he caught sight of their guest and he bent over him, gripping his shoulder. "Easy, honey, she's a friend. I think."

"What do you want?" Alex asked, his voice low and rough. Mihai stirred at the sound, sitting up abruptly with a choked off gasp. Alex said something soothing and Mihai sat back, watching Meera suspiciously, poised as if to run—IV pole, handcuff, and all.

Meera gave him a reassuring smile over her shoulder and turned back to Oren. "Anouk sent me. I'm here to help you guys."

"By writing a 'sensational' news article about us?" Oren asked.

"By getting your story out there," Meera said evenly. "Think about it. The more people know about this, the more they talk about it, the more 'sensationalized' it is, the better it will be for you when it comes to trial."

"Court of public opinion," Oren said slowly as understanding dawned. "Anouk, you mad genius."

Alex was looking back and forth between them, his face blank. "Oren, what—"

Oren dropped a kiss on his lips. "I'll explain later. Do you trust me?"

"Always," Alex said instantly.

"That's good," Oren said, smiling at him. "Can you tell Meera your story?"

Alex's face clouded and he hesitated, looking at Meera, who smiled at him.

Finally, though, he drew a breath and sat up, facing her. "My name is Alexandru Costea. My brother Mihai and I—"

Oren held him as Alex told his story again and Meera took notes, her pen moving rapidly across the page.

When Alex got to collapsing outside Oren's house and waking up in his bathroom, Oren patted his hand.

"I'll take it from here, okay?"

Alex nodded, clearly grateful, and Oren began talking. He took Meera through everything, from fleeing the house to roughing it in the woods to barely making it to the hospital, and then to their marriage.

"You got married because you knew he'd be deported otherwise?" Meera asked.

"That was why I initially suggested it, yeah," Oren admitted. He took Alex's hand, feeling the delicate structure of bone and ligament, running a thumb over Alex's knuckles. "But then I realized that I'd fallen in love with him."

Mihai cleared his throat, the sudden noise in the quiet room making them all jump, but said nothing.

"That's good," Meera said, writing quickly. "That's romantic, it'll be a big hit."

"I'm not trying to be romantic," Oren said, nettled. "I'm just telling you how it happened."

Meera flashed him a distracted smile. "I know, but I have to present this in the best possible light, and this… this will help."

Oren subsided and Alex squeezed his hand. Mihai glowered from the opposite bed but said nothing.

"If we're lucky," Meera said, still writing, "this will go viral. The more people share your story, the better it will be. But don't talk to anyone but me, okay? Now, what happened at the house?"

"I'm not sure how much I can tell you," Oren said. "Considering someone died and all."

"Good point. Tell me everything up to that, then."

Oren obeyed, stopping when they were snatched. Alex had drifted back to sleep somewhere during the trip back to Cheyenne. "I don't think I should give the details of the house just yet," Oren said, and Meera nodded, swiveling to Mihai.

"And this is the famous brother, huh?"

Mihai crossed his arms, a gesture already beginning to seem familiar to Oren, and said nothing.

Meera's eyebrows rose a fraction. "Would you like to make a statement?" she prompted.

Mihai shook his head silently.

Oren said nothing, and Meera rose, pocketing her notebook.

"Thanks for your time," she said in a low voice. "I'll be in touch." She smiled at him and disappeared on soundless feet.

17

Detective Nguyen woke them up the next morning, hands on her hips and an unholy storm in her eyes.

"You talked to the press," she hissed.

Oren's eyebrows went up. "In all fairness, you didn't say *not* to, Detective. Meera's… a friend."

"I didn't say you *could*, either!" Nguyen snapped. She blew her bangs off her forehead as Alex turned his face against Oren's chest and Mihai bristled. Nguyen noticed and took a deep breath. "No more statements to the press. That goes for all three of you."

"Is the article any good?" Oren asked.

Nguyen tossed her phone in his lap. "See for yourself."

Today I want to tell you an unconventional love story.

Oren Asher and Alex Costea are very much in love. It shows in the way Oren holds Alex, how he puts himself between Alex and anything that might be a danger. It shows in the way Alex turns instinctively to Oren for comfort and the way they touch each other, gentle and caring.

Alex and Mihai Costea were born to poor parents in the town of Vaslui, Romania. They were inseparable growing up, getting into and out of trouble as a unit. So Alex didn't even think twice when he learned their parents had sold Mihai into sex slavery to cover their debts. He went after his brother, to rescue him, but he couldn't get him out alone. So he did the unthinkable. He willingly entered the world of sex trafficking, all so that his brother would not be alone.

Mihai is about seventeen, with brown hair, dark green eyes, and a brittle bravado that hides a wounded soul.

Alex is nearly twenty-two, tall and far too thin, blond haired and brown eyed, and he speaks in a soft, halting accent as he describes how he and Mihai were allegedly 'broken in' by Andrei Sokolova, the head of the notorious Russian mob located in downtown Cheyenne.

"Not in our town!" I hear you cry.

Believe it, reader—the police confirm that Andrei Sokolova has been "a person of interest" in their investigations for a number of years, but they've never been able to get any charges to stick.

Until Alex managed to escape, taking with him a thumb drive containing all of Andrei's clients—insurance, of a sort, for his plan to return and trade the drive for Mihai once Alex was healed.

Alone, starving, bruised and broken in body but not in spirit, Alex fled Cheyenne, his wild flight leading him to Oren Asher's doorstep, where he hoped to steal some food before continuing his journey.

Instead, he collapsed outside Oren's door, where he was found as Oren was taking out some trash.

Oren takes up the tale here as Alex falls silent, pressing his face against Oren's shirt and closing his eyes.

Oren Asher is a name many of you are perhaps familiar with, considering he's a prominent local artist in high demand, making amazing creations out of driftwood and found objects. He values his privacy, though, keeping to himself in the house he built outside town.

Oren is short and sturdy, his Hispanic heritage evident in his brown

*eyes and black hair. He is quick to
smile, even with all he's been through
recently, a dimple appearing in his
cheek when he does. I have the feeling
that he's only half-aware of me, so
focused on Alex is he.*

*He talks quickly, the faintest of
accents shaping the curve of his words,
as he tells me about how he took Alex
in and cared for him during the
snowstorm, tending his injuries and
learning his story.*

OREN PUT the phone down without reading
more. "Wow."

"You could say that," Nguyen snapped,
grabbing the phone. "Not another *word* to the
press, you hear me?"

"What's the reception been?" Oren asked.

Nguyen hesitated. "Pretty solidly in your
favor. People seem to think it's really goddamn
romantic, for some reason." She gestured and
Selene stepped into the room. "Now, it's time
for you to go back to your room."

Alex clutched Oren's sleeve. "Oren, no—"

Oren covered his hand. "We talked about
this, remember? We knew they'd separate us. I
won't be far, sweetheart." He glanced up.
"Detective, can you—I know you can't
promise anything, but some kind of reassur-
ance would be nice."

Nguyen took a step forward and Alex met her eyes. "Alex, I don't know what's going to happen, but I can tell you this much —you and Mihai will not be sent back to Romania, nor will Oren be extradited to Texas, until a judge reviews the case here. And even if one of those things happens, you'll see each other again before then. Okay?"

Alex turned back to Oren, tears in his eyes. "*Te iubesc*, Oren," he whispered.

"I love you too," Oren managed, cupping Alex's face. "I'll see you really soon, okay?" He looked up to see Mihai watching him, eyes unreadable. "Take care of him," he said, and Mihai nodded once, sharply.

"SO YOU'RE A HERO, APPARENTLY," Selene said in the hall.

Oren tilted his head to look at her.

Selene smiled. "Everyone's talking about the article that dropped this morning. You two falling in love like that, you risking death to help him and trying to save his brother? It's an incredible story."

"It's not a story," Oren said, hunching his shoulders. "It *happened*." He glanced back at her again. "Selene... could you do me a favor? Could you check in on Alex, maybe take him notes that I write to him? He's not going to take this separation well."

"I'll see what I can do," Selene said, the

corner of her mouth curving up in a conspiratorial smile.

ALONE IN HIS ROOM, with a police officer posted outside his door, Oren picked up the phone and placed a collect call to a number he hadn't used in years.

"Hello?"

Oren couldn't help his smile. "Hi, Mom."

18

HE STOOD BEFORE THE JUDGE, wearing a suit that didn't quite fit, hands clasped in front of him, his mother, Alex, and Mihai sitting in the front row of the courtroom behind him. A glance over his shoulder showed Oren that Flora had her arm around Alex, bracing him as they waited for the judge, who was leafing through the papers on his desk.

Finally, he put them down and fixed Oren with a gimlet eye. "This has been one hell of a case, Mr. Acevedo."

Oren gulped.

Judge Winters continued without waiting for a reply. "The media coverage alone has been ridiculous. Seems like everyone from three states around has an opinion on this. I had the governor of Texas on the phone just last night and I don't mind telling you, he's not pleased either."

Oren said nothing, ducking his head and trying to look contrite.

Judge Winters sighed and ran a hand over his thinning white hair. "Leaving aside you skipping out on your parole, it seems to me that you've been a model citizen the entire time you've lived in our state. You've never been in trouble with the law, you've boosted the local economy with your art, and you seem to have reformed your life in many ways."

Oren glanced at Alex again, sending him an encouraging smile and then facing forward to meet the judge's eyes.

"As for your husband," Judge Winters said, "he is in this country illegally, as is his brother. However, there is clearly nothing for them in Romania, and he has indicated—quite strongly, I might add—that he wishes to remain with you. Because they have both cooperated so fully in taking down Andrei Sokolova's operation, and because I find myself convinced that this really is a love story, however unconventional, I am hereby granting them United States citizenship and acknowledging your and Alexandru's union officially."

Oren turned, smiling so widely his face hurt. Alex was smiling too, a hand pressed to his mouth and tears in his eyes as Flora hugged him close. Mihai watched Alex, something almost like a smile on his face, and didn't move. Oren swiveled to face the judge again.

"Thank you, Your Honor."

"Don't thank me yet," Judge Winters said. "There's still the matter of your parole violation. I am in agreement with the governor of Texas on this, I might add. I'm sentencing you to time served, plus one year in a federal penitentiary." He brought the gavel down with a sharp crack.

Oren caught his breath and nodded. "Yes sir."

Judge Winters was watching him closely. "You will be eligible for parole in six months, with good behavior. Something tells me you'll be home with your family in time for Thanksgiving."

"I have every intention of it, sir," Oren said clearly.

"Say goodbye," the judge said, picking up his papers. "You're leaving for Texas immediately."

Oren turned as Alex stood up and Flora handed him his crutches. They met in the middle of the room and Oren pulled Alex close, feeling the tremors shuddering through his thin frame. He could hear camera shutters clicking as the reporters in the room tried to get a good angle, but Oren didn't care.

He eased away, putting a finger under Alex's chin and lifting it up until their eyes met. "Hey," he whispered.

Alex's lips trembled. "Don't leave me, Oren."

"I'm not, baby, I swear," Oren said, cupping his face. A tear slid down Alex's cheek and Oren wiped it away with his thumb. "You're gonna go with my mom and Mihai, okay? She's going to take really good care of you both, spoil you rotten, tell you embarrassing stories about me when I was a snot-nosed brat. And I'll call you every week, and write to you every day. Will you write to me?"

Alex nodded, more tears sliding down his cheeks. "Every day," he said, his voice thick. "*Te iubesc*, Oren. Please… be safe."

"I will, sweetheart," Oren promised, and pulled him down into a kiss.

He lost himself for a long, stolen moment in the sweetness of Alex's mouth, his hands clutching Oren's ill-fitting coat and the soft breaths that feathered across his cheek, but finally someone touched his shoulder and they broke apart with a regretful sigh.

Oren looked for his mother, a few steps away. "Take care of him, Mom."

"Of course," Flora said simply. "We'll see you soon."

Oren looked at Mihai next. Mihai tipped his chin up, looking back, and Oren couldn't help the smile. "You're an incredible kid," he said softly. "I see why Alex loves you so much."

And then the guard was there, pulling Oren's arms behind his back and cuffing him, turning him toward the door. His last sight was Mihai and Flora with their arms around Alex, tears on his face as they watched him leave.

19

SIX MONTHS LATER

"Let's go, Acevedo, your ride's here."

Oren looked up, startled. The guard standing in the doorway of his cell was one of Oren's favorites, an older man named Larry, belly sagging over his duty belt and the hair he had left graying and sparse.

"Is it that time already?"

Larry rolled his eyes, hitching up his belt. "Like you haven't been counting the seconds. Come on, let's go."

Oren grinned as he scrambled to his feet and hurried to shove his few belongings into the bag Larry held out.

It had been six months since he'd seen Alex without guards watching their every move, six long months of serving his time in the Huntsville prison, keeping his head down, writing to Alex every day and calling him every week without fail. Alex visited once a month, sometimes flying in alone and sometimes accompanied by Flora and Mihai.

Alex sounded good during his phone calls too, telling Oren all about living with Flora, who'd immediately set about mothering them both properly, feeding them constantly and fussing over them in a way that Alex at least clearly enjoyed.

Oren quickened his pace.

"Slow the hell down, they're not going anywhere," Larry snapped, and Oren forced himself to match Larry's ambling speed as they made their way down the cold concrete hall toward the front of the prison.

"Hey, Acevedo, you leaving us? What's the matter, we not good enough for you?" Sixpack was resting his muscled forearms on the bars of his cell door and grinning at him, gold tooth glinting.

Oren blew him a kiss, making him laugh. "Not that you're not great fun, Six, but I've got something better waiting for me."

Sixpack saluted him. "Good luck out there, amigo."

Oren grinned and sped up again.

"Goddammit, Acevedo, I don't get paid enough to chase after your ass," Larry complained, but he moved a little faster, scanning his badge and pulling the door open as the buzzer sounded.

In the front office, Oren impatiently signed every form shoved at him, craning his neck for a glimpse of Alex. The waiting room was barely visible from where he was standing; only a few empty chairs in his line of sight.

"Missed one," the jailer said, tapping the form in front of Oren with her pen.

Oren signed yet again and finally, his belongings were handed over in a large plastic bag. Oren opened the bag and fumbled through his folded clothes until his hand closed around what he'd been looking for. He ran his thumb over the silky wood, smiling, and then pulled the carving out and shoved it in his pocket.

Larry pulled the heavy door wide and gave him a lopsided smile. "Don't let me see you back here, Acevedo."

"Larry," Oren said fervently, "I hope I never see you again."

Larry's laugh was the last thing he heard as the door slammed shut behind him. Oren looked around the waiting room, searching for blond hair, but he saw his mother first, inspecting the snack machine with a suspicious scowl.

"Mom!" he said and she turned, her face lighting up.

"Orlando, *hijo*, come here!"

Oren laughed and scooped her into his arms, smelling her familiar scent, lilies and flour from the tortillas she made by hand every morning. He took a deep breath, closing his eyes as memories rushed over him.

"Ben always loved your tortillas," he said.

"I remember," Flora said, patting him on the back. "Always stealing them, the little shit.

Alex does the same thing. I guess you have a type."

Oren couldn't help the laugh as he let her go. When he looked up, Alex was standing behind Flora, looking nervous.

"*Buna*, Oren," he said.

Oren swallowed hard. "Hey," he managed. "You look so good."

Alex had gained at least thirty pounds and there was color in his cheeks, his hair freshly cut and looking silky soft where it fell forward over his high forehead.

"Oh, go hug your husband," Flora scolded, shoving Oren forward.

Oren took a step and Alex met him halfway, arms opening to wrap around him. Oren buried his face in Alex's throat and took a shaky breath, gripping him tight.

"I missed you so much," he whispered.

Alex's arms tightened and then he let go to cup Oren's face in both hands, bending to kiss him. Oren went up on tiptoe and their lips met in a soft, sweet slide. Alex tasted like apples and smelled like home, and Oren didn't fight the tears that sprang to his eyes.

When they separated, Alex thumbed a tear off Oren's cheek. "Don't cry."

"Happy tears," Oren said, smiling and blinking them away. "Where's Mihai? Did he decide to sit this out?"

"I'm here," Mihai said, materializing behind Alex's shoulder. He'd gained weight too, expression still reserved as he regarded

Oren, but his skin clear and eyes bright. "I would not miss this."

"I asked him to come," Alex admitted, giving Mihai a smile over his shoulder, and Mihai's face softened as he returned it.

"Come on, let's go," Flora said, herding them toward the door. "You two lovebirds can catch up in the car instead of blocking traffic in here."

Alex was walking without a limp, Oren was delighted to see, his gait swinging and loose, and he gripped Oren's hand tight as they walked, like he planned on never letting go again.

Oren felt like he was walking on air himself, lightheaded with happiness, and he couldn't stop smiling as they crossed the parking lot, hazy with summer heat, and reached Flora's car.

"Back seat, you two," Flora said as she slid behind the wheel and Mihai got in the front seat.

Oren obeyed, only letting go of Alex's hand long enough to get into the car and then grabbing it again. A smile flickered across Alex's mouth and he stroked Oren's knuckles as Flora began to drive.

"What time is our flight?" Oren asked.

"No flight just yet," Flora said. "Alex has something to show you first."

Oren looked at Alex, who smiled and offered no explanation.

"So how are things with your therapist?" Oren asked instead.

Alex lit up. "Good," he said. "She is so nice."

"It's a treat listening to them jabber at each other in Romanian," Flora said over her shoulder.

"And the video conferencing works?"

Alex nodded. "Da. Yes, I mean. I use Flora's computer, she set up it all for me."

"Mihai, how do you like her?"

Mihai lifted a shoulder. "She's fine," he said without turning his head.

Oren caught Alex's eye and Alex sighed.

"He likes her a lot," he said. "She's been good for him." *Sorry*, he mouthed.

Oren squeezed Alex's hand and leaned forward to address Flora. "Mom, are you sure you won't consider moving to Cheyenne when my parole is up? I'll build you a house of your own close to ours and everything."

Flora snorted. "Maybe when I retire. Not just yet. Besides, I'll have six months with you getting underfoot first. I'll probably be well and truly sick of you by then anyway." She grinned at him in the mirror.

"Say the word and I'll get the foundation poured," Oren told her, grinning back.

IT WAS several hours before Flora took an exit on the outskirts of San Antonio, which Oren spent whispering to Alex and occasionally leaning across the seats to kiss each other.

Oren looked up as the car slowed. "Mom?" They were nowhere near home.

"You didn't think we were going to drive all the way home, did you?" Flora asked. "That's an eleven hour drive, you *must* be insane. Mihai and I are going to the airport, and *you*—" She pulled off into the bay of a hotel and parked.

Alex was already in motion, pushing the car door open and scrambling out, extending a hand to Oren, still sitting in the backseat.

Flora turned to face him. "It wasn't my idea," she said. "But I was happy to bankroll it. I don't want to hear from you for the next three days, understand?"

Oren swallowed guilt. "I'm sorry," he said, his throat tight. "I left you for so long, and I know you worried—I wanted to write more, but I couldn't risk it—"

"I knew you'd come back when you were ready," Flora said. She reached over the seat and took his hand. "I won't pretend I wasn't hurt when you called and said you were *married* and could your new husband and brother-in-law come live with me while you went back to prison, but Orlando—*Oren*... I get it. And I fell in love with Alex five minutes after meeting him, I understand why you did everything for him." She squeezed his hand.

"Wait, so whose idea was it?" Oren asked. "Alex?"

"No," Alex said from outside the car.

Mihai cleared his throat.

"Are you serious?" Oren said.

"Alex, let me help you with the bags," Flora said, and hopped out of the car.

Mihai swiveled in his seat until Oren could see his profile. He was staring at his lap, lips pursed as if trying to figure out what to say.

"I hated you," he finally said.

Oren flinched but nodded. "I know."

"I wanted to think you took my brother," Mihai continued. He looked up before Oren could respond. "I told myself you did, that you stole him from me."

"I'm sorry," Oren whispered. "I didn't mean to—"

"What they did to us, in that place," Mihai said as if he hadn't even heard him, "it will stay with us the rest of our lives. You know that, yes? Our therapist says it will be ours forever. That we will never… be truly free of it, of the… horror."

Oren's throat was tight but he managed a nod.

"I have never seen Sandu so happy as he is when he's talking to you." There were tears in Mihai's eyes. "I thought I would never hear him laugh again. But then I would see him on the phone with you, and you would make one of your stupid jokes—truly, they are *so* stupid—"

Oren couldn't help the laugh, even choked with tears. "I know, I'm sorry, I can't help it—"

"You gave me back my brother," Mihai

said, and the tears spilled down his cheeks. "And I repaid you by hating you."

"No." Oren reached for him without thinking, and Mihai took his hand over the seat. "No, kiddo, that's not what you did. And it'd be okay if you *had*. I'm sorry, I'm so sorry all this happened to you, that we couldn't get to you sooner, that you went through it in the first place. I wouldn't blame you if you hated and distrusted me forever. All that matters is you're safe."

Mihai dashed tears away with his free hand. "I wanted to give you this. To thank you. For my life, and my brother's life, and for what you did."

"I keep telling everyone, it was all Alex," Oren said, but he was already reaching out to pull Mihai into an awkward hug with the seat between them. "Thank you," he said against Mihai's glossy hair, and Mihai sniffled and patted his arm.

WHEN OREN SLID from the car, Alex's smile was blinding. He leaned down to say something soft to Mihai through the window and press a quick kiss to his cheek, and then he straightened, holding out a hand to Oren.

"We have nice room. *A* nice room. Come, I want to show you."

He towed Oren into the lobby of the gracious old building and Oren stared around him in wonder at the vaulted ceilings and marble floors. Alex didn't give him much time to take it in, though, too busy tugging Oren between clumps of tourists to the elevator.

There were several other patrons in the car, so Oren didn't kiss Alex, who was so excited he was practically fizzing, bouncing on his toes in place.

On the fifth floor, Alex grasped Oren's hand again and took him down the richly carpeted hall to a room that he unlocked with a key in his pocket.

Inside, the walls were papered in a rich yellow, the four-poster bed covered in a blanket of green and complementing yellows. Two mahogany desks stood against the far wall, bathed in light from the high windows.

Alex looked suddenly shy. "Do you… like it?"

Oren turned and caught him around the waist, pulling him close and making him yelp. "It's amazing," he said against Alex's neck. "Almost as amazing as you."

Alex laughed, his head falling back, and Oren took the opportunity to explore the long column of his throat.

"God, I missed you," he murmured, kissing the smooth skin under his lips.

"I am sorry I could not visit more," Alex said, his voice suddenly serious. "I wanted to, but—"

"Planes aren't cheap and driving is worse," Oren said, easing away. "And it wasn't too bad, with the phone calls and letters. Oh, I have a present for you!"

Alex looked startled. "For me?"

"It's not much," Oren said, digging in his pocket, "and I didn't have time to wrap it, not that it'd look any better wrapped, I'm a shit wrapper, anyway here—" Aware that he was babbling, he shoved the carving into Alex's hands.

Alex turned it over, running his finger over the grain of the wood, following the whorls. Oren had left the features blank intentionally, the slim figure of a boy leaned over a smaller boy and sheltering him with his arms showing more through suggestion and the natural curves of the wood than explicit detail.

Alex took a step back, drawing Oren with him, so he could sit down on the bed, his mouth working and tears in his eyes. "It is me and… Mihai?"

Oren settled next to him. "Remember I started working on it back in the house, but I wasn't sure what it wanted to be yet? Well, it finally told me."

Alex ran a thumb over the featureless face of the smaller figure. "Thank you," he said after a minute, lips trembling. "Thank you, Oren. I love it. I love *you*."

"Still?" Oren teased. "After all this time?"

"Always," Alex said. "Always forever, Oren."

Oren caught his breath and leaned in to kiss him. Tongues slid against each other, noses bumping and Alex's breath puffing warm and soft over Oren's cheek. What started out slow and sweet gradually changed to hungry and wanting, and Oren could feel himself hardening as they fell backward onto the mattress and Alex slung his leg over Oren's hips to pull him closer.

"Ah—*fuck*," Oren managed after a minute. "Alex, honey, are you sure—"

Alex nodded, his lips kiss-swollen and his eyes dark with desire. "I want you, Oren. Please? If—" He hesitated. "If you want me. Is okay if you don't, I don't—"

Oren rolled to a sitting position and Alex followed suit, looking suddenly unsure.

"I want you too," Oren said, taking his hands.

"But—" Alex ducked his head and looked at Oren's fingers in his. "You said no sex. You said kissing was okay but not—if you don't want… it's okay—"

Oren squeezed his hands and Alex faltered to a stop, taking a ragged breath.

"It took me a long time to figure out what I was, how I identified," Oren said. Alex watched his face, eyes somber now. "I… I wanted sex with Ben, but not at first. I thought he was beautiful, but there was nothing physical there, you know? But then we became friends, and then best friends, and one day I realized I wanted him so much I burned with it."

Alex nodded. "You loved him."

"So much," Oren whispered, throat thick. "He was—yeah. Anyway, I was young and stupid and didn't think much about it, and then everything… happened. It was years before I really thought about it again. I started reading about it. I think I'm asexual, at least… sort of? It's called demisexual, sometimes. I don't want sex until I have a bond with someone. Which is why, with you—"

Alex's eyes kindled with shy hope. "You do want me?" he whispered.

"So much," Oren said, smiling at him, and Alex leaned forward to wrap his arms around Oren's neck.

"I want you too," he said against his ear. "I didn't think I would, at first. But you would never hurt me, and I love you so much, and I want—I want everything with you. Yes? Please, can we?"

"Far be it from me to argue with you having your wicked way with me," Oren said, and kissed Alex's nose before rolling away to stand up on the far side of the bed. He pulled his shirt off as Alex propped himself on his elbows to watch and Oren couldn't help flexing a little.

"You are… what is word?" Alex asked. "Bigger. Muscles?"

Oren couldn't help his laugh. "Not much to do in prison but work out and keep my head down—enjoy the muscles while they're here, because a few months of my mom's cooking and I'll have lovehandles again."

"I like all of you," Alex said seriously. "No matter what." He patted his own belly. "I am almost fat, me. Flora's fault." He flashed a grin at Oren.

Oren laughed outright and kicked his

pants off to crawl back on the bed. "You're *adorable* is what you are, pal. How come you still have clothes on?"

Alex sat up and Oren knelt to help him pull his shirt off. He stopped to admire once his upper half was bare. Alex's skin was soft and smooth, marred by a few scars here and there, but whole and unbroken, and Oren bent forward to press a kiss to Alex's breastbone, no longer concave.

"Almost fat, my ass," he murmured, and felt the laughter that vibrated through Alex's frame. Oren smiled and kissed his way down Alex's chest, stopping at his waist and sitting up to reach for his belt.

Alex watched as Oren tugged the belt free and unzipped his pants, lifting his hips so Oren could pull them down.

"Is it creepy to tell you I've jacked off to the thought of this?" Oren asked, looking up.

Alex smiled, wide and delighted. "I have too," he admitted. "I have wanted you for so long, Oren—"

"You have me, gorgeous," Oren said, crawling up Alex's long body. "What would you like from me?"

"All of you," Alex said, reaching up and pulling Oren's head down. "All of you."

Oren lowered his body, feeling Alex's hard length pressing against his belly as they kissed, and he couldn't resist rolling his hips in a slow, filthy grind that had them both gasping.

"You think you could fuck me?" he whispered.

Alex's eyes went wide. "You want me to—"

"God yes," Oren breathed against Alex's throat. He kissed his way down his chest again, teasing his nipple into a hardened nub as Alex gasped, his back arching. "Are there… supplies?"

They found massage oil in the bedside drawer and Oren popped the cap. The scents of rosewood and vanilla filled the room, but before he could pour the oil on his fingers, Alex sat up with shocking speed and grabbed the bottle.

"I want—can I?"

Oren gulped. "Yeah, of course." He flipped over and lay down on the bed, face against the mattress, spreading his legs and listening to Alex settling between them.

One slick finger touched his hole, and Oren canted his hips so that the tip slid inside.

Alex spread his free hand across the jut of Oren's hipbone, anchoring him, and kissed the curve of his buttock as he pushed his finger deeper.

Oren sighed, relaxing into the intrusion.

"Okay?" Alex asked.

"Mm." Oren slanted a smile at him over his shoulder. "More than. Keep going."

Alex smiled back and added a second finger as Oren hardened under his attentions, until he was leaking onto the bedspread and rocking back against Alex's hand.

"Yeah," he gasped as Alex found his

prostate and rubbed and fireworks went off behind Oren's eyes. "Oh *god*, Alex—" He tried to work a hand between himself and the bedspread, but Alex caught his arm, pulling it away from his body.

"No."

"*Please.*" Oren was finding it difficult to form words, and then Alex added a third finger. Oren bucked at the stretch and burn, almost sobbing.

"Is good?" Alex's English was deserting him, Oren noticed distantly.

"*Yes*, but please, can I touch—"

"Not yet."

Alex found Oren's prostate again, sliding over it, and Oren decided he wasn't going to survive. He was so hard it *hurt*, a constant throbbing that pulsed in time with Alex's fingers, and still Alex stretched him, slow and methodical and merciless.

"I'm ready," Oren gasped when he couldn't bear it any more. "Please, baby, *please*—"

Alex pulled his fingers out and curved himself over Oren's prostrate body, laying butterfly kisses up his spine until he was on top of him, lowering himself until he could nip Oren's ear.

"I'm gonna die," Oren informed him, and Alex huffed a warm laugh.

"You want me to fuck you?" he murmured, rubbing their cheeks together.

"Pretty sure that's what I've been *begging* you for," Oren retorted.

Alex nipped his ear again, sharper this time, and Oren jerked.

"Ah—*fuck*—come on, Alex, what do you want from me?"

Alex hummed and dropped a kiss on Oren's cheek before levering himself up and catching Oren's knee. "Over," he directed.

Oren obeyed, rolling to his back. A glance assured him that Alex was just as aroused as he was, his shaft flushed a dark red. Oren's mouth watered.

"Next time," Alex said. He moved closer, running his hand up Oren's thigh. "So beautiful," he murmured.

"Alex Costea-Acevedo, I swear to God, if you don't *get a move on*—"

Alex laughed, his head falling back and pure joy pealing forth, and despite Oren's state, he couldn't help but laugh with him, exulting in the sight of his lover so cleanly *happy*.

Still. Oren hooked his heel around Alex's hips and pulled him forward. Alex caught himself with a hand on either side of Oren's shoulders, laughter cutting off but a smile lingering.

"Thank you," he said, bending his head to kiss him.

Oren arched up into it, arms snaking around Alex's neck and his tongue delving greedily inside Alex's mouth. "Please fuck me," he whispered against Alex's lips.

"*Bine*," Alex said, and sat up on his heels. He scooped up the massage oil and slicked himself thoroughly and then guided himself to Oren's entrance.

Oren gasped as Alex pressed in, stretching and filling him to overflowing as he slid home in a slow, controlled glide.

"Oh, Jesus," he choked, clutching handfuls of the bedspread. Alex hilted himself, flattening a hand on Oren's stomach, and a tense, waiting silence fell over the room.

Alex sucked in air. "Okay, Oren?"

"Better than, so much better than, come on, baby, don't make me beg."

"But I *like* it," Alex said, teasing rich in his voice, and Oren opened one eye a slit and glared at him.

"At some point, we're going to have to discuss this seriously toppy kink you've been hiding from me," he said. "Right now, I'm in dire need of a good fucking."

Alex laughed again, delight vibrating through him, and began to move. He set a steady rhythm immediately, pulling almost all the way out and back in, punishingly strong thrusts that had Oren's eyes rolling back in his head as the head of Alex's cock dragged over his prostate and more fireworks went off.

"Alex," he panted. "Please, can I—"

"No," Alex said, and Oren gave serious thought to crying in sheer frustration, but then Alex's hand was wrapped around his cock and he was stroking in counterpoint to his hips, thumb gathering up the pre-come as he swept it over the tip.

"I'm gonna—'m gonna come," Oren

choked, drowning in sensation, the familiar tightening in his balls his only warning before the lightning gathered at the base of his spine burst outward.

He came in heavy, desperate pulses onto his stomach, bliss shivering along his nerves, and dimly aware that Alex had driven home, dropping his face to Oren's throat as he spilled deep within him, hips jerking in needy, grace-less time to his own orgasm.

Alex collapsed on top of him and Oren reached a wavering hand up and stroked his silky hair, floating on endorphins and joy.

It was a while before Alex stirred and pulled out with a groan and Oren sighed at the loss as Alex rolled off the bed and padded naked to the bathroom. When he came back, it was with a warm, wet towel to wipe Oren down in quick, gentle movements.

Oren cooperated dreamily, half-asleep, groping clumsily at whatever part of Alex was close, and Alex avoided his pawing with more laughter.

"Come back to bed, *catâr*," Oren begged.

Alex tossed the towel into the bathroom and obeyed, gathering Oren in close and tugging the end of the blanket over both of them.

"I love you, *dragă*," he whispered in Oren's ear.

"What does that mean?" Oren said, rubbing his nose against Alex's collarbone.

"Darling," Alex said, pulling him closer.

"Dearest, sweetheart. It's all—everything I feel for you."

Oren kissed Alex's clavicle. "Luckiest bastard alive," he mumbled, and Alex's chest shook with silent laughter.

THERE WAS SO much to do. After their honeymoon, they would go home to Flora and Mihai. Alex and Mihai were both studying for their high school diplomas, and Mihai was already talking about colleges— although he wasn't willing to consider looking outside Wyoming just yet. Oren was sure his mother had a list as long as her arm of things she needed fixed around her house. He still had orders to fill, and he'd be able to start work on them in Texas.

And when they got back to Cheyenne, he had a house to rebuild, this time with an extra bedroom for Mihai.

So much to do. Oren smiled to himself, Alex's heart thumping steadily against his ear. He couldn't wait to get started.

ACKNOWLEDGMENTS

Aaliya, who was there for me when I wrote this book. Even when I doubted every word, you never lost faith in it and me. Tell Gary I love him. Chris is okay too, I guess.

Sarah, who listens to what I want out of a cover and somehow magically produces either exactly what I was envisioning or something even better. I don't know how you do it but I live in awe.

Ioana, my Romanian cultural advisor. This book really does exist because of you. Thank you for lending me your lovely language and helping me make Alex and Mihai as real as possible. Any mistakes are my own.

And all my readers, on Tumblr, Twitter, and Facebook—thank you for embarking on these journeys with me and keeping me so excited to give you more. I'm grateful for you all every day.

ABOUT THE AUTHOR

Michaela Grey told stories to put herself to sleep since she was old enough to hold a conversation in her head. When she learned to write, she began putting those stories down on paper. She resides in the Texas Hill Country with her cats, and is perpetually on the hunt for peaceful writing time.

When she's not writing, she's watching hockey or blogging about writing and men on knife shoes chasing a frozen Oreo around the ice while trying to keep her cat off the keyboard.

Tumblr: greymichaela.tumblr.com
Twitter: @GreyMichaela
Facebook: www.facebook.com/GreyMichaela
E-mail: greymichaela@gmail.com

Want to find out when her next book comes out? Sign up for her newsletter here or follow her on Amazon here

ALSO BY MICHAELA GREY

Beloved Scars

Broken Halo

Broken Rules

Broken Trust

Broken Promises

Blindside Hit:

A Toronto Wolverines Novel

Odd-Man Rush: A Seattle Kingfishers Novella

Keep reading for a sneak peek of *Blindside Hit,* available now and the beginning of *Cold Stone Heart,* coming soon from Michaela Grey!

BLINDSIDE HIT

CENTER ICE WAS A WELL-KNOWN gathering place for hockey players, and it catered to that demographic shamelessly, with signed pictures and jerseys of famous players on the walls and huge flat-screen TVs in every corner, playing whatever game was on. During the off-season, they played highlight reels, Liam told Etienne, towing him to a table in the back.

A cheer went up at the sight of the three of them and Etienne stopped dead in shock at the sight of most of his team gathered there, all grinning at him.

"*Why?*" he finally managed.

Liam clapped him on the back, hard enough to knock him forward a step. "Because you don't know how to have fun, and we're gonna help with that."

Rudy pointed to a chair, a smile on his dark features. "What are you drinking?" he asked as Etienne settled beside him with a nod to Logan.

Etienne shrugged. "I don't care."

"You may be a lost cause," Johnny said. "Tibs, get us a pitcher of beer, would you?"

Liam headed for the bar and Etienne looked around the table. Next to Logan was Broussard, and Theo, unfailingly as sunny as Broussard was sour. Jax and Wyatt were in the corner talking, but they spared a moment to wave at Etienne.

"You guys really all came out just to make sure I'd have a good time?"

Rudy gripped his shoulder, grinning at him. "You work too hard, Tenny. You need to relax."

"I can relax!" Etienne protested.

The faces around the table didn't look convinced. Liam returned with two pitchers of beer and flopped down beside Johnny, who absently curved his hand over the nape of Liam's neck.

Rudy followed Etienne's gaze to Johnny's hand and cleared his throat. "Ah, Tenny...."

"They told me before they press-ganged me," Etienne said.

"And you're okay with it?"

Etienne almost laughed at the echoing of his own question. "Seeing as I am too, yeah."

Rudy relaxed and glanced around the table, meeting everyone's eyes individually. Each in turn nodded as Etienne watched, confused. Finally Rudy turned back to Etienne.

"In that case, you should know most of us here aren't straight either."

Etienne's eyebrows shot up. "Sorry, what now?"

"Me, I'm bi," Rudy said.

"Knew I was gay when I was twelve," Johnny offered.

"I don't know what I am," Liam said. "I like hot people."

"Kinda ace," Theo said, shrugging. "But when I do feel… whatever, it's guys."

"Fuck off," Broussard snapped.

Theo sighed. "Robert."

Broussard glared. "Whatever. I'm gay, I guess. Probably."

Logan signed something. Rudy watched his hands and turned to Etienne.

"He says he's gay. Also, that reminds me, I need to get you and the rookies enrolled in the next sign language class at the university. Logan will go with you, give you some extra signs you'll need to know to be able to talk to him."

Etienne nodded and Logan gave him a smile surprising in its sweetness.

"Hey, so what's the deal with Coach?" Etienne asked Rudy.

Rudy's eyes tightened and he took a sip of beer.

"Come on," Etienne said. "He almost never comes out of his office unless it's to yell at us. You do all the actual play-making and strategy sessions. What's up with that? Why is he even employed?"

Rudy sighed and set his beer down. "It's not something I can talk about. Don't cross him, though."

A shiver of unease slid down Etienne's spine. "Why not?"

"Just trust me," Rudy said.

Someone roared with laughter from two tables away, making everyone turn and look. A group of men were clustered together around another, standing and holding his mug of beer in one unsteady hand.

"Hey," Johnny said, eyes narrowing. "Isn't that...."

"Adam Caron?" Etienne said. "Yeah, I think it is." He couldn't look away. Adam was even better looking in person than on the ice, his dark hair falling over a high forehead into big, dark blue eyes. He was grinning at something one of his companions had said, those full, kissable lips curving into an infectious smile that somehow lightened Etienne's mood just by looking at it.

"Is that—are those the fucking *Freeze?*" Broussard said, craning his neck to see.

"So it would appear," Theo said. He sounded faintly starstruck. Logan patted his shoulder, lips twitching. "I've only ever seen Adam skate," Theo said. "God*damn* he's hot. Ow!" He rubbed his thigh as Broussard glared at him. "I'm allowed to think other guys are hot, Rob. It doesn't mean I've suddenly stopped thinking *you're* hot."

"Speech, speech!" someone shouted.

Adam laughed and shook his head.

"Didn't he just get called up permanently by the Wolverines?" Johnny asked.

"That must be why they're celebrating," Liam said. "Let's invite them over." He was out of his chair and heading for the other table before anyone could stop him.

"Gosh, I love how impetuous he is," Johnny said into his beer. "That never backfires *ever*."

Liam was talking to the other group, which turned as one to inspect their table. Rudy and Johnny waved as Etienne tried to figure out how to make a run for it, but it was too late. All six men were on their feet and following Liam back over.

"Rudy!" Adam said, eyes sparkling. Rudy jumped to his feet to greet him.

"I honestly wasn't sure you'd remember me," he admitted.

"Have you *seen* you skate?" Adam demanded. "Of course I remember you!"

"Adam and I attended a training camp together last year," Rudy told the table.

"And you're just now telling us this?" Liam said, sounding betrayed.

"Join us?" Rudy asked Adam.

For several minutes, it was a mad scramble of finding chairs and rearranging to make sure everyone had room enough to sit down, and when the dust settled, Adam was sitting next to Etienne, crammed in so tight their legs were pressed together under the table.

"Hi," Adam said, offering a hand. "Adam Caron."

Etienne stifled a laugh. "I know who you are. Etienne Brideau. I play for the Thunder."

Adam nodded sagely. "I've heard your name."

"You have?"

Adam had clearly worked his way through more than a few beers. His eyes were glassy, cheeks flushed, and he swayed ever so slightly when he moved.

"Mm-hmm," he said, leaning toward Etienne. "The new left wing. Footwork like Astaire and a right hook like Ali. You're going places." He grinned. "Like me. I'm going places. I'm going to the Wolverines. Did you hear?"

"Yeah," Etienne said. His head spun, and he didn't think it was the beer he'd barely touched. Adam Caron—*the* Adam Caron— had heard of him. Had heard *good* things about him. He dragged himself together. "Sorry, uh—congratulations, man, that's amazing news."

Adam's smile widened. "Thanks. I'm celebrating."

"I can tell," Etienne said, fighting a smile.

Adam leaned in, lips to Etienne's ear. "I saw you watching me. Do you want to celebrate with me?"

Etienne froze. He hadn't heard right. There was no way Adam Caron had just hit on him. But Adam was smiling at him from an inch away, the intent clear in his eyes.

"Isn't there... someone else you'd rather, uh... celebrate with?" Etienne managed.

Adam pouted, pushing out that full lower lip. Etienne wanted to suck on it. He tore his eyes away, clearing his throat.

"You don't want to?" Adam was asking.

"Oh, I do," Etienne said, and Adam's smile returned, bright enough to light the room. "But I just—" He gestured helplessly, at the people around them and then himself. *So many better options*, he was trying to say, but he couldn't figure out how to put it into words.

Adam put a hand on Etienne's thigh, making him jump. "My place is just a block away," he breathed.

Somehow, Etienne found himself following Adam from the bar as his friends laughed and shouted encouragement.

Blindside Hit is available now!

COLD STONE HEART

SNEAK PEEK

CHAPTER ONE

Isaac Summers was too damn stubborn to die.

He stumbled down the street, his arms wrapped around his waist, vaguely certain at least three ribs were cracked. One eye was rapidly swelling shut, his vision blurry and indistinct out of the other, and there was a slow, dull ache between his legs. He knew, somewhere deep in the back of his mind, that he wasn't going to make it to a hospital or to the shelter before he collapsed. Blood was dripping from a cut on his forehead and he swiped at it clumsily, missing a step and catching himself on the iron railing beside him before he fell.

He looked up, blinking and trying to focus on the huge brownstone in front of him.

Maybe the owners wouldn't mind if he spent the night on their front porch. Maybe he could slip inside and they wouldn't even know he was there.

Isaac pushed open the gate and staggered down the path, weaving drunkenly toward the front door. He'd almost made it when the blackness dragged him under.

CHAPTER TWO

He woke up warm and dry, his whole body a solid scream of pain, blinking back to consciousness slowly. There was an extra warm spot on his hip, and it seemed to be vibrating. Isaac opened one eye and stared up at an ornate ceiling.

"Don't move," a voice said.

Isaac turned his head toward the sound, trying desperately to focus and biting back the agony. There was a dark-skinned man sitting beside the bed he was in, leaning forward with concern written all over him. Isaac stared at him for a minute.

"Where... am I?" he slurred.

The man frowned. "You're in my house," he said. "My name is James. I found you outside my front door."

"Thanks, but I can't... fuck you... right

now," Isaac managed. "Maybe… in a day… or two…"

James pulled back, revulsion clear on his face. "What the fuck is wrong with you?" he demanded.

Isaac huffed a humorless laugh. He could feel the blackness tugging at him again, dragging him down with sticky fingers. "Where do I st—" He was unconscious before he could finish the sentence.

Sign up for Michaela's newsletter here
or follow her on Amazon here
to find out when Cold Stone Heart is available!